"WHAT THE HELL IS THAT THING?"

The chariot was round. A flat-seeming disc about thirty feet in diameter. Spurts of flame were shooting out of the rear end of it. There was a sound, too, an odd humming that the disc made.

The chariot continued to drop. It couldn't be more than fifty feet from the ground now.

"He's going to crash!"

Stevenson scrambled to his feet, abandoned his duffel bag and went running across the desert in the wake of the falling disc.

Smitty's friend could not know he was running to his death. But it was a death that would not go unnoted. It would bring Justice Inc. into action to probe a danger worthy of the talents of THE AVENGER.

the Avenger

BLACK CHARIOTS

By Kenneth Robeson

WARNER
PAPERBACK
LIBRARY

A Warner Communications Company

WARNER PAPERBACK LIBRARY EDITION
First Printing: November, 1974

This Warner Paperback Library Edition is published by
arrangement with The Condé Nast Publications Inc.

Cover illustration by George Gross

Warner Paperback Library is a division of Warner Books, Inc.,
75 Rockefeller Plaza, New York, N.Y. 10019.

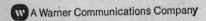 A Warner Communications Company

Printed in the United States of America

CHAPTER I

Death from the Sky

Ten people had seen the chariots in the night sky that week.

The eleventh person to see one died.

That was because of two breakdowns. Just one of those things, both breakdowns happening at the same time. Only a coincidence, but it killed Lieutenant Ralph Stevenson.

There was a hot wind blowing across the Southern California desert that night. The kind of rasping wind that took all of the moisture out of you, made you feel as though you were part of the desert itself, dry and gritty.

The car, a 1933 coupé he'd borrowed from a cousin in Glendale, didn't like the wind, either. It rattled, gasped, and wheezed as it moved along the straight flat night road.

The shadowy desert stretched away, perfectly

flat, on all sides of Lieutenant Stevenson. Standing off there in the desert were the shaggy Joshua trees, all spiky elbows they seemed.

"What is it, must be five years," Stevenson, a big bony young man of twenty-six, was saying to himself as he drove toward his destination. "Sure, it must be five years since I've been out this way. I was at Cal Tech then; a bunch of us drove out for the weekend. Yeah, and I met that crazy blonde who said she'd come out to Hollywood to be an ice skater in the movies, like Sonja Henie."

That made him think of another girl, a more recent part of his life. He'd thought he would be spending this leave with her. But then that letter had—

The old coupé gave a long, mournful sigh and ceased to function. It rolled, ever slower, to a stop, shivering.

"Hey," Stevenson said aloud, "we're due in Manzana tonight, Old Paint. Let's keep 'em rolling." He clicked the ignition off, turned it on, and tried to get the old machine to start.

Nothing happened.

Stevenson fiddled with the choke and tried the starter once more.

The car remained dead.

"Well, let's put some of my vast technical knowledge to work." He stretched out of the car and hoisted up one side of the hood.

There was no other traffic on the road. It was a little after 10 P.M., according to the lieutenant's watch.

"Very smart, Loot," he said to himself, nodding at the smoking, hissing radiator. "Damn thing sprang a leak and I didn't even notice."

6

The car might be fixed, but not by him. Not with the simple tools in the tin box under the seat, not on this side road twenty-six miles from the town of Manzana and, so it appeared to him, a thousand miles from anything else.

"Well, I'm still in uniform. Maybe I can thumb a ride. Most people are pretty good about that," he reflected. "But what people?"

No lights showed anywhere. No house lights, not one approaching car in either direction.

"Twenty-six miles to the town." Stevenson sat on the running board. "I could walk it in . . . maybe three hours or so. There's bound to be somebody going my way in that time."

Standing, he took the keys out of the car, and his duffel bag. He had some civilian clothes in that. He was intending, during the week he'd be at the Manzana Lodge, to get a lot of use out of those clothes.

"Nothing like a little cross-country march to limber you up." He slung the bag over his shoulder.

He was looking forward to this week at the desert resort. Not the way he'd been looking forward to getting together with . . . well, no use dwelling on that. Two of his best friends had managed to shift their schedules around so they could all rally here at the same time. Dipper Willet, whom he'd known since high school, and Smitty. Smitty'd been a friend of his ever since they'd met in New York before the war. Funny thing about Smitty. He looked big and dumb, like maybe a circus strongman, but he was really an exceptionally bright guy. Maybe even something of a genius in his field of radio electronics.

Stevenson was smiling over his use of the word genius when the chariot flew over.

At this point in time, although nearly a dozen people had seen the chariots and over half had reported it, there had been almost nothing in the newspapers or on the radio about them. There was, as we'll see, good reason for that.

Even so, people talk. All across the desert country rumors were spreading about the chariots and what they might be. Most people who'd seen them called them the black chariots. The things weren't black, actually, more a dark gray shade. You would have hardly been aware of them up there in the night if it hadn't been for the tail of yellow-red fire they gave off as they streaked overhead, blotting out the stars as they passed low over the desert.

This one, the one that would cause Lieutenant Stevenson's death, was coming in extremely low. Not more than two hundred feet above him.

He heard it first, and looked up. Instinct made him throw himself flat out on the desert road. But this wasn't a strafing plane.

"What the hell is that thing?"

The chariot was round. A flat-seeming disk about thirty feet in diameter. Spurts of flame were shooting out of the rear end of it. There was a sound, too, an odd humming that the disk made.

The chariot continued to drop. It couldn't be more than fifty feet from the ground now.

"He's going to crash!"

Stevenson scrambled to his feet, abandoned his duffel bag, and went running across the desert in the wake of the falling disk.

CHAPTER II

A Long Wait

The electric fan behind the hotel desk rattled as it spun. There was very little breeze produced by the ancient mechanism, not enough to riffle the obviously false hair of the clerk who was slouched a few feet in front of it. He was a heavyset man, in his fifties, leaning with both elbows on the knotty-pine registration counter.

From outside came the enormous gasp of the last bus from Los Angeles. The fat clerk straightened, wiped perspiration from his forehead and neck, and adjusted his wig.

A big man, a giant almost, came in out of the warm, windy desert night. He was carrying two heavy-looking suitcases as though they weighed nothing at all. Dropping the luggage in front of the desk, the big man said, "I got a reservation."

The clerk watched the door for a moment,

wondering if any more guests for the Manzana Lodge were going to come in. The glass door didn't open again. "Yes, sir," he said. "Name, please?"

"Smitty," said Smitty.

"First name?"

The giant hesitated. His full name was Algernon Heathcote Smith, but he never used it. Nor was he very fond of anyone who did. "A.H. Smith," he told the clerk finally.

"Ah, yes, here we are. Mr. A.H. Smith of New York City." The fat man had located a small file card in a dented tin box. "Yes, we've got you in room 213, right between your two friends."

Smitty smiled. "That sounds okay," he said, glancing at the clock on the wall. It was almost midnight. "Kind of late, but I guess I can knock on their doors when I get up there."

The fat clerk, as he turned the hotel register toward Smitty, said, "I don't believe Lieutenant Stevenson has checked in as yet, sir."

"Huh?"

After consulting another card from his tin box, the clerk said, "No, although he was due to arrive between ten and eleven this evening, according to his original reservation."

Smitty looked over his shoulder, at the dark outskirts of the desert town. "Well, these days and a guy in the Army, nobody arrives right on the button any more. When he does show up, no matter how late, tell him to stop in."

"I surely will."

Smitty signed the register, then took one more look outside. "You say Dipper Willet is here?"

"Yes, Mr. Willet arrived late this afternoon.

10

You'll find him in room 214," replied the clerk. "I don't suppose you'd like me to carry your bags to your room?"

"Naw, I can manage." He held a huge hand out.

The clerk dropped a room key into it. "I hope you'll enjoy your stay in the desert, Mr. Smith. Some people, especially folks from back East, think our climate's just too darn dull. Dry and hot, dry and hot . . . that's about all it ever is."

Smitty nodded. "Be sure to tell Lieutenant Stevenson to let me know when he gets in." His big fingers closed over the room key, and he picked up his luggage. Walking toward the stairway, Smitty frowned.

With his training and background he should be the kind of person who operated entirely on facts and figures. But once in a while Smitty got a hunch. He had one now, about his friend Ralph Stevenson. He kept on frowning.

"There's a war on, Smitty, nothing is on time any more, nobody." The young man in the redwood chair was small and dark.

Smitty seemed even more gigantic in contrast. "Naw, Dipper, I got a feeling something's wrong. Look, it's almost one A.M. Ralph should have got here by now."

Dipper—his real name was Charles Willet—drew a half-circle on his knee with the base of his highball glass. "Working for Justice, Inc., has made you overly suspicious," he said. "Now myself, after three long years with TechNamics, Ltd., over in Hawthorne, I've lost all my imagination. That's great, because with no imagination, you never worry."

Smitty sat down on the edge of his bed, studying his friend's face. "You're not happy over there, huh?"

"Why shouldn't I be? TechNamics pampers me, pays me an immense salary," he replied, "and I'm helping the war effort."

"You guys doing defense work there?"

Dipper said, "Forget I mentioned it, Smitty. I'm not supposed to talk about it. A slip of the lip can sink a ship, and so forth."

"A guy with your brains," said the giant, "you ought to be happy."

The small young man laughed. "Still the same old Smitty. You've got the same view of the world as Shirley Temple."

"Maybe so."

"And you're happy, Smitty?"

"Sure." He stood up and walked to the window to stare once more down at the dark desert. "Do you know which way he was coming? Maybe we could go—"

"Haven't any idea," said Dipper. "Ralph called me yesterday at work and mentioned something about visiting relatives before he met us for the big reunion."

"Which relatives? Do you know where they live? We could maybe call them."

Dipper shook his head and took a sip of his highball. "No idea. Ralph may have mentioned the name, but it sure didn't stick in my head."

Smitty pressed one big hand against his stomach. "Something's wrong."

"Turn off your imagination," Dipper advised. "We'll be seeing Ralph any minute now."

But they never saw him again. Not alive.

CHAPTER III

"Don't Ask Questions!"

The highway patrolman was leaning way back in the swivel chair, reading a true detective magazine. A single fly was sneaking across a patch of morning sunlight on the desk top toward the glazed doughnut on the coffee saucer. "Help you?" the patrolman asked. He read to the end of the paragraph and steepled the magazine next to his cup. "That Dillinger was something, wasn't he?"

Smitty came closer to the desk. "I'm trying to locate a friend of mine," he said. "I understand you guys found an abandoned car near here early this morning. Maybe it's his."

The patrolman looked at his coffee cup, the doughnut, the skulking fly, but never at Smitty. "What did you say your name was?"

"It's Smith."

"Oh, yeah?"

Smitty got out his wallet and flashed his identification at the man. "What can you tell me about that car?"

The patrolman looked at the wall clock, which jumped ahead a minute, then at his cup. "Who exactly are you looking for?"

"This is no way to get answers," said Smitty. "I ask a question, then you ask one back." He put his huge fists on the desk edge and leaned toward the smaller man. "My friend's name is Lieutenant Ralph Stevenson. He was supposed to meet us over in Manzana last night. He didn't. Early this morning I started calling around. Now we're following up leads. What about that car?"

The highway patrolman picked a slip of paper from his desk top. "Car belongs to a Nick Carr of Glendale."

"Yeah? And where is Mr. Carr now?"

"We're checking into it."

"Was it an accident?"

"We don't believe so."

"Where's the jalopy now?"

After a few seconds the patrolman said, "Over in Bockman's Garage."

"You don't mind my having a look at it?"

"No, you can look all you want." He reached for the phone. "You go on over, it's down the street two blocks to your left, and I'll call Bockman to tell him it's okay." When Smitty was in the doorway, the highway cop added, "I don't think this has anything to do with your friend."

The giant said nothing.

14

Bockman was old, way up in his seventies. He gave the impression when he bent down to squint under the pickup truck he was working on that he might never be able to rise up. "What?" he said.

"I'm the guy the patrol phoned about," repeated Smitty. "I came to look at the car they found in the desert."

"Okay, okay." The old man pointed into the garage at his left. "Got her in there, the coupé."

Smitty started for the shadowy oil-smelling garage. Old Bockman followed him.

"I know," said Bockman, "what got him."

"Huh?" Smitty turned and eyed the ancient mechanic. "Got who?"

"Whoever it was who was driving that car," he said. "Oh, they don't like to talk about it, the cops, but everybody knows, anyhow."

"What do you mean? Something out in the desert?"

Bockman jabbed a gnarled forefinger skyward. "Something up there."

"What—planes, you mean?"

"Nope, they ain't planes. Haven't seen one yet myself, but they ain't planes." The old man wiped his palms on the legs of his tattered overalls. "Not that I go along with Prester Ambrose, but—"

"Who's Prester Ambrose?"

"A crackpot. But he might, just might, be right about them chariots."

Smitty put a big hand on the old man's thin shoulder, trying not to let his exasperation show. "What are the chariots?"

"Black chariots—those that've seen them call

15

them that. Black chariots, from lord knows where. They come swooping down like—"

"Mr. Smith?"

A man was standing out in the bright morning glare. He was carrying a raincoat over his arm and a briefcase in one hand.

Smitty couldn't make out his features. Blinking, he walked over to him. "Yeah?"

The man was young, neat, affable. "Like to talk to you."

Smitty cocked his head. "You got that look. You government?"

The cleancut young man showed him his credentials. "Don Early, from Washington, D.C.," he said. "Heard of you."

"Yeah, and I've heard of you, too, Early," growled the giant. "You're always butting into our cases."

Early smiled his boyish smile. "Depends on your point of view," he said. "Walk over to my car."

"You got something to tell me?"

Early's face changed; all traces of the smile vanished. "Afraid it's bad news."

"About Ralph?"

Early stopped on the sidewalk beside his 1938 Plymouth. "He's dead."

Smitty reached out, steadying himself against the car. He felt as though he'd fallen from a great height. "No, he was going to—"

"That is the car he was driving, in there," Early went on. "He was found about a quarter-mile from it."

"What killed him?"

"We don't know yet."

16

A terrible look crossed the big man's face. "Somebody killed him, though?"

"He was murdered, yes."

"How? Who did it?"

"His body is being examined now."

"You got to know whether it was a knife or a gun or what."

Early put a foot on the running board. "You're on vacation, aren't you?"

"Yeah, we were all going to get together, Ralph and Dipper and me."

"You're not in California on Justice, Inc., business?"

Smitty scowled. "Up till now I wasn't. But the way you're talking, Early, makes me—"

"I know you'd like to do something, find out who killed him," said the government agent. "But I'd like you to leave this to us. There are certain things involved that I can't go into. Don't investigate, don't ask questions."

"I'm not going to promise anything like that. Ralph was my friend and I—"

"This isn't like the other times. You won't be tolerated."

"Tolerated? Hell, we cleaned up all of those other cases for you."

"Only a friendly warning . . . now."

Smitty took a step back. "Ralph just died, and you're on top of this already," he said, slowly. "That means you were probably already out here in the desert. This is part of something bigger, ain't it?"

The agent said, "Might be."

"Is it the black chariots? Is that what you're digging into, Early?"

Early reached out and got hold of the car's door handle. "Got your address, where you're staying. I'll let you know what I can about Lieutenant Stevenson." He climbed into his auto.

"I won't quit," promised Smitty as the car drove away.

CHAPTER IV

Wayfarers

She was lost.

The flickering midday desert surrounded her, made her feel like a very small pebble on a very large beach.

Jennifer Hamblin was fairly positive she'd taken the right turn, back at the crossroads. But now, literally in the middle of nowhere, she was starting to have her doubts. This couldn't be the way to the Manzana Oasis resort.

Everything around her was brown, shades of earth brown. The land, the strange trees, the rocks, even the birds.

Jennifer slowed her car as the road grew even narrower. Dust and grit flew up, and pebbles clattered against the fenders. The roadway climbed, up through sandy orange-brown cliffs.

"Better turn around, Jenny," the blond girl told herself.

She was stubborn, though. She'd picked this road, and she was going to stick with it. Eventually it might lead to the resort.

Stubbornness. That was—admit it, Jenny— what was behind this whole trip. A trip all the way across America to the Southern California desert. Well, she'd always been stubborn and impulsive, doing things no polite Boston girl ought to do. Uncle Val had always called her . . .

"I know he's out here," she said aloud. "He has to be."

The narrow road continued to climb, higher into the rocky hills.

A proper Boston girl would have accepted the facts. Uncle Val was probably dead. He'd been missing for over a year. No one, not the police or the FBI, had found one trace of him. Nothing to indicate where he'd gone when he'd left his office on campus that night. He'd walked away, into nowhere.

"But I know something they don't know," she said.

What Jennifer knew, coupled with one single story in the back pages of the *Boston Herald*, had prompted this trip. The story had been about the first sightings of the disk-like black chariots over the desert. One small story had made it out across the country before all mention of the black chariots was stopped.

The car, huffing, crested the hill. There in front of her rose a high fence. It cut across the road, blocking any further progress.

"I guess I'll have to concede that this isn't going to turn into the right road after all."

Far beyond the wire fence, shimmering like a heat mirage, stood a castle. It was vast, pale yellow, with towers and spires thrusting up into the bright day. On the fence itself were bolted two signs, neatly lettered. The first read: THIS FENCE GOT ENOUGH ELECTRICITY TO KILL YOU DEAD! KEEP AWAY! The other sign announced: I DON'T SEE NOBODY. (Signed) OLD MAN GUPTILL.

Jennifer, her stubbornness taking over, pulled her car over to the roadside. Getting out of the machine, she walked over to the electrified fence. "I don't see why they can't at least tell me how to get to the Manzana Oasis."

The girl halted a foot in front of the wire gate and cupped her slender hands to her mouth. "Hello, can anyone help me?"

Five seconds passed.

Then someone started shooting at her with a high-powered rifle.

He stood on the street corner, an umbrella in one hand and a shepherd's staff in the other. He was long and thin, wearing a homespun robe. His beard, blue-black in color, reached nearly to his waist. In his deeply tanned, weathered face his pale blue eyes glowed. "We are all wayfarers," he shouted at the few people who had stopped to listen to him, "all wayfarers on the thorny path of life." He pointed his staff at his audience, most of whom were slouched in the shade of a barbershop awning. "I bring you good news, friends, yes, good news. The journey will soon be over. Yes, soon over, and we will be wayfarers no more. We will be dwellers in a far better place—"

"Hope it's cooler than Manzana," remarked one of the listeners.

The bearded man went on. "Yes, friends, a better place than this, a better world. You have the solemn word of Prester Ambrose that this old world will soon be over. How do I know? Ah, I know, friends, because the signs have been sent. Signs in the heavens, which I have witnessed with my own eyes. Yes, I have seen the black chariots, and I know, friends. The end is nigh. Will you be ready?" His head suddenly bent, indicating his sermon had finished. From within his robe he produced a pewter mug which he set on the hot sidewalk next to his sandaled foot.

Two of those who'd been listening came forward to drop coins into the cup; the rest shuffled away.

All but one man. He remained in the shadows of the striped awning, watching Prester Ambrose. He stepped into the light now. "I'd like to talk to you," said Smitty.

The robed man bent and picked up his cup. It rattled.

Smitty dug out a quarter and plunked it into the mug. "I want to know about the black chariots."

"They are a sign, friend, a sign sure and true that the longed-for end is—"

"I don't want the philosophical angle," interrupted the giant. "I want specific details on what the damn things look like."

Prester Ambrose scanned him with his pale blue eyes. "Come to the Sacred City tonight," he said. "A small donation, say twenty bucks, wouldn't be out of order." He bowed to Smitty and walked away, umbrella held high, staff tapping the pavement.

CHAPTER V

Desert Treasure

Jennifer ran, getting her car between herself and the rifleman. Another bullet went whistling overhead.

She was on the passenger side of the car. Cautiously she took hold of the handle. "Locked."

And the key in the ignition. So she would have to work her way around the machine. All the way around, then dive into the driver's seat and back away from here.

"Even if he doesn't shoot me," she thought, "there's a good chance he'll plug one of the tires. Or maybe even the gas tank."

There weren't too many alternatives. She had to get away. Old Man Guptill, whoever he might be, didn't seem to be the kind of person you could reason with.

"If you get out of this mess, Jenny, you're really going to have to—"

"Hey there, girl!"

On the other side of the fence stood a white-haired man. He was big, wide-shouldered, wearing a dirt-streaked white suit. He held a rifle under his right arm.

"I lost my way," she called.

"Can't you read, girl?"

"I didn't touch your fence."

"The part about Old Man Guptill don't see anybody. Means what it says."

"I have absolutely no desire to see him, whoever he is." Jennifer decided she could step out from the protection of the auto. "What I want is someone to tell me how to get to the Manzana Oasis."

"Other road is what you want, girl."

"You mean back at the crossroads?"

"Left-handed road."

"But I did take the road on the left."

"Damnation, girl don't you even know your left from your right?"

"Of course I do."

"Go back and give it another try."

Jennifer took several steps toward the fence. "You must be the one who shot at me."

"Dang right I am."

"Would you be Old Man Guptill himself?"

"I might," answered the old man. "Or I might only be one of the dozen guards Old Man Guptill got on his payroll. Fierce bunch, they are."

She walked nearer. "What is it you're guarding? I know some people value their privacy a good deal, but—"

"Where you hail from, girl?"

"Boston."

Scratching his standup white hair, the old man said, "You mean to stand there and tell me they ain't never heard of Old Man Guptill in Boston, Mass?"

"Perhaps someone has," replied the blond girl, "but I haven't."

"Well now, girl, Old Man Guptill used to be nothing more than a drifting prospector, about nine cents short of owning one thin dime," said the old man. "Then one day, so the story goes, he struck it rich. Found a cache of gold that'd been hidden in the desert by the Spanish way back when."

"And you built this fortress with the money?"

"Some of the dough Old Man Guptill used to construct himself a showplace. Since he'd roamed the desert all his miserable days, he built his mansion right here in the desert."

"The fence, and the guards, that's to protect the treasure?"

"Everybody wants Old Man Guptill's treasure."

Jennifer said, "Thank you for the directions, and the story, Mr. Guptill."

"Never said I was Old Man Guptill."

Jennifer reached the resort at two o'clock that afternoon. The Oasis consisted of three large adobe and tile buildings and a dozen smaller cottages built around a huge oval swimming pool. Trees, ferns, and flowering bushes walled in the Manzana Oasis's nine acres. Despite its name, the resort was eight miles this side of the town of

26

Manzana. It was, like a real oasis, the only spot of green for miles around.

An attendant in a scarlet coat came trotting toward Jennifer's car as she turned into the parking area.

"Afraid there are no vacancies, miss," he told her.

"I have a reservation."

The young man put a hand on the window edge. "We're full up, I'm pretty sure."

"If you don't mind, I'll go in and find out for myself."

After a few seconds the attendant said, "Certainly, miss. I'll park your automobile for you."

"Thanks."

The lobby of the Oasis, all tinted glass and turquoise tile, was extremely cool, almost chill. Behind the curving tile-fronted registration desk was a small stiff man in a polo shirt and blazer.

"Yes?"

"My name is Jennifer Hamblin. I have a reservation."

"I'm afraid not, miss. We have absolutely no vacanies at the Oasis."

"But the reservation was made by a travel agency in Boston, and confirmed."

The clerk sighed sympathetically. "These days, with so many wartime stresses, miss, it's really no longer possible to be certain of anything. I assure you we have no reservation for you, and no accommodation."

"Don't you even have to check to find out?" she said. "Look won't you? My name is Jennifer Hamblin."

"There's no need to look because—"

"One moment, Joel." A thin dark man had stepped out of a rear office behind the desk. He beckoned to the clerk.

"Excuse me, miss."

Jennifer pretended to be studying the chill lobby, although she was really trying to hear what the two men were saying. She had no luck at that.

"I'm terribly sorry, Miss Hamblin," said the returning clerk, "I find we do have your reservation, after all. If you will simply sign the registration card, I'll summon a bellboy."

The dark man remained in the doorway, watching Jennifer.

She gave him a tentative smile.

He turned away, went into the office, and closed the door.

CHAPTER VI

Sacred City

The twilight was full of barking dogs. Smitty could see their silhouettes all along the side of the winding hill road. The big man was driving Dipper's car. His friend considered an interview with Prester Ambrose a waste of time and had remained at the inn.

"He's taking this whole thing pretty light," Smitty said to himself.

Another dark dog showed in the dusk. A hunched, growling police dog. A thin young man in overalls was restraining the anxious animal with a hand clutching its heavy collar.

The two of them were standing in front of the plank fence against which the road ended.

Stopping the borrowed car, Smitty got out. "I've come to see Prester Ambrose."

"You a convert, friend?" The young man

asked, his voice harsh and nasal. "All converts are always welcome here at Sacred City. Other kinds of folks, though—"

The bristling dog snarled and tried to get free to attack Smitty.

"It's a business deal," said Smitty. "I'm buying something."

"Oh, yeah, he told me about you." Struggling to keep the dog with him, the young man walked to the gate in the wooden fence and, one-handed, pulled it open. "Come on in, mister."

Smitty, ignoring the snarling dog, walked onto the grounds of Sacred City.

The city covered about three acres. It was set in a small gulley in the rocky hills ten miles beyond Manzana, a collection of ramshackle wood houses, forlorn trees, and dry weedy ground. There were more dogs on this side of the fence, smaller and less vicious. Most of them didn't even bother to bark at the passing giant. Lights were on in half of the ten houses, from kerosene lamps since there was no electricity.

Seated on the top step of the porch of the largest house, his staff across his knees, was Prester Ambrose. "Welcome, friend, to Sacred City," he called through the dusk. "I know full well that to your eyes this must seem a poor place indeed. It is not always appearance, but rather purpose, which will smooth our way into Eternity. Thus far my followers live humbly here in Sacred City, but someday—"

"Doesn't much matter, does it? You were saying when I caught your sermon in Manzana that the world's about ready to end."

"True, friend, true," said the bearded man. "I've seen the signs in the heavens."

30

"Yeah, that's what I want to talk about."

"You brought the dough, friend?"

Smitty sat down on a lower step and handed him two ten-dollar bills. "Describe these black chariots to me."

Prester Ambrose, folding the bills away in his robe, said, "I witnessed only one, friend. It was indeed strange and wonderous to behold. Aye, it screamed through the air like an avenging—"

"Whoa!" said Smitty. "Skip the poetry, I want specifics. Details."

"It's not an airplane. At least, not in the conventional sense," said Prester Ambrose. "Obviously it's an aircraft of some kind, but it's round, without any visible wings. Shaped like a plate, or more accurately, two plates stuck together." He pressed his palms together. "Roughly twenty-five feet across the middle, and up on top there's a kind of bubble. I didn't get too good a look at that part of the thing. Could be that's where the guy who pilots the thing sits, or it might be where they got their gadgets in case the thing is some kind of radio-controlled drone. Out the back it was spitting fire."

"What—an exhaust, you mean?"

"Not sure, friend. The thing was traveling pretty fast."

"What about propellers?"

"Weren't any, no sound of them, either."

"Whereabouts did you spot this chariot?"

"Between here and town. I was making a little pilgrimage into Manzana, just about a week ago. I was on foot, since I don't believe in automobiles."

"How low was it flying?"

"Few hundred feet, no higher."

31

"What's it made of?"

"Can't be certain, friend. Might be metal, might be some kind of plastic."

Smitty asked, "They didn't try to communicate with you, harm you?"

"No, friend, I went my way, and they went theirs."

Smitty remained seated on the porch step for nearly a minute, silent. "Anything else you can tell me?"

Prester Ambrose said, "I can give you some advice, friend. Which is, forget about this whole thing. You're bucking something pretty strange."

Rising up, the giant said, "It's not the first time."

He was five miles from Manzana when they made their move.

The dark sedan, running with its lights out, came roaring out of a side road.

"Hey, you dope!" hollered Smitty when he realized the other car was barreling straight for him.

He twisted the wheel, and the machine went squealing in a jagged arc. Smitty took it too close to the edge. The car jumped from the road and went rocketing down across the gravel shoulder.

"This ain't no accident."

He hit the brakes to avoid smashing into a giant many-armed cactus.

A chattering filled the night. The back window exploded, scattering jagged shards of glass all around.

"Oh, boy, a tommy gun!" Smitty grabbed his door open and threw himself out into the desert.

Another burst of machine-gun fire cut across the darkness. Several of the surrounding cactuses were dismembered.

On his belly, Smitty got as far from the abandoned car as he could.

"Over there!" shouted a throaty voice. "I seen him move."

The machine gun chuttered once more.

A joshua tree was cut in half about fifteen feet from Smitty.

"Okay, they ain't got me spotted very good." From a pocket of his coat the giant extracted a small glass pellet. Eyes narrowed, he watched the night road. "There!" He rose for only an instant to fling the glass pellet.

His toss was fairly accurate. The pellet smashed on the roadway beside the man with the submachine gun.

"What the hell!"

Blackness, blackness deeper than any night, surrounded the gunman and the two others who shared the road with him. This was the special gas used by Justice, Inc. When it connected with air a cloud of impenetrable black was produced.

Hopping to his feet again, Smitty hotfooted it across the desert and then up onto the road. "The gunsel should be right about . . . here," he said to himself, reaching into the swirl of blackness.

"Something's got—"

The giant's hands closed around the throat of the man who'd tried to gun him down. He yanked him out into the night air.

"He's here!" the gunman gasped.

Holding him by the neck with one hand, Smitty chopped the machine gun from the man's hands. "I don't like them things." The weapon clanged on the road.

Smitty lifted the thin, pale-faced man up high. "You the ones who killed Ralph Stevenson?"

"I don't know nothing about—" The man went stiff. There had been a tiny puffing sound and he had jerked his body.

"I asked you . . ." Smitty realized he was holding a dead man. A shot, silenced, had come out of the blackness.

Now he heard a motor sounding He dropped the dead man and jumped aside.

The black sedan came shooting out of the swirl of gas. In a few seconds it was far off on the night road.

Shaking his head angrily, Smitty knelt and searched the dead gunman. There was absolutely nothing in his pockets. "Damn," said the big man, "a dead end."

CHAPTER VII

Teamwork

Josh Newton got up out of the chair he'd been slouched in. He wandered to the windows of the Justice, Inc., office. Spring had reached Manhattan, and the street below was bright with warm morning sunshine. The short block was called Bleek Street. It was all owned, though very few people knew this, by the Avenger.

Putting his hands in his trouser pockets, the black man made a random circuit of the large office. "Doctor said it won't be till next week," he said to himself. "But I got a feeling . . ."

The door opened, and a lanky sandy-haired man came in. "Ye dinna look yer usual relaxed self, Josh," observed Fergus MacMurdie.

"I got a feeling that—"

The phone on the desk rang. Mac was closest, so he answered. "Aye? Ah, fine, and yourself, lass?" Beckoning to Josh, he handed him the phone. " 'Tis for you."

"Hello. Oh, yeah, hello, Rosabel. You sure? You're sure, okay. You wait right there, you hear? No, you won't take a cab. You wait for me. Bye, honey." He hung up and ran for the door. "Looks like the baby's going to arrive today, and not next week. I got to get Rosabel to the hospital."

"Give the lass m' love."

"I had a feeling . . ." Josh barged into the corridor, barely missing the arriving Nellie Gray.

The little blonde watched him go clomping downstairs before she went into the office. "Rosabel?"

"Appears the wee bairn is arriving a few days ahead of schedule," said the Scot.

Smiling, Nellie took a chair. "That's wonderful," she said. "I hope it's a girl, because I know that's what Rosabel—"

"What was that object that flashed by me as I tottered up here?" Cole Wilson, grinning, sauntered into the room.

" 'Twas Josh," said MacMurdie. "Looks like he's to become a father this day."

"I'm sure it'll be a boy, since that's what Josh—"

"Honestly!" said Nellie, with a demure snort.

"Oh, it's you, pixie," said Cole. "I didn't notice you there, you being so diminutive."

"What's that all over your shoulders?" the blonde asked him. "It's a little late for snow, even in a city with as crazy weather as New York."

Cole lowered himself, slowly, into a soft chair. "Must be confetti. I'm actually just returning

36

from a farewell party for an old fraternity brother of mine. He's a captain in the Army and—"

"Good morning." Richard Henry Benson came into the room. He was young, of average size, dark-haired. There was something about his pale eyes that made you think he might be much older than he looked. "We have something new to work on."

"Smitty," said Cole.

The Avenger glanced at him. "What makes you say that, Cole?"

"Every time one of our little band goes on a vacation, he falls into a whole slough of trouble. Mac encountered witches, warlocks, and Old Nick himself when he tried to spend a few quiet days in New England; Nellie was almost the main course for a werewolf when she attempted a holiday visit to her relatives; and when I made a seemingly harmless pleasure jaunt to the film capital, we ended up tussling with zombies. So I figure . . ."

Benson nodded his head as he took his place behind his desk. "Three men tried to gun Smitty down last night," he told them. "He called from southern California early this morning."

Mac leaned forward in his chair. "What were the skurlies up to?"

Steepling his fingers, the Avenger said, "One of the two men Smitty was supposed to meet out there in the desert was killed before they ever got together."

"That's terrible," said Nellie. "Poor Smitty."

"From the details Smitty gave me over the phone," continued Benson, "what happened to his friend is much more than just a highway killing." He proceeded to tell them about Lieuten-

37

ant Stevenson, Prester Ambrose, the black chariots, and the presence on the scene of Agent Early.

"Whoosh," commented Mac when Benson had finished, " 'tis a fine stew Smitty has got himself into."

Cole asked, "What about the chariots, Richard? You don't share the desert prophet's public view that they're unearthly in origin, do you?"

"No, Cole, and I don't think they're late arrivals for an Orson Welles broadcast."

"Charles Fort," said Nellie.

"Eh?" said Cole, cupping a hand to his ear.

"Haven't any of you read Charles Fort's books? He maintained, I'm not sure how seriously, that Earth has been visited by extraterrestrial ships for years, probably centuries."

"Farfetched," said Mac.

"At this point," said the Avenger, "we don't know what these flying disks are. We do know, howe er, that Don Early is already out there investigating."

"Meaning," suggested Cole, "that we're talking not about aliens from another planet but from another country, mayhap."

"The possibility that these chariots are involved in some kind of spy operation does arise," said the Avenger.

"How about Smitty's friend?" asked Nellie. "How does his death tie in?"

"He may have, by chance perhaps, got too close to one of these chariots," said Benson. "Smitty was allowed to view the body; he says there were no marks on it. So far, Early hasn't told him the results of the autopsy."

38

"Ray guns," said Cole. "That's what Martians use."

Nellie scowled at him.

The Avenger said, "This affair interests me. We'll go out to California."

"Agent Early will nae like that," said Mac.

"You and I, Mac," said Benson, "will check into the place where Smitty is staying, in Manzana. Cole, you and Nellie book yourselves into one of the desert resorts, someplace out of town."

Mac stretched up. "Ye heard Josh's news, Richard?"

"Yes, so we won't include him on this excursion."

"It's going to be a girl," Nellie said, still scowling at Cole.

"Would you care to make a small wager?"

CHAPTER VIII

The Mirage That Wasn't

Another breakdown brought Smitty a little closer to the solution.

It was late afternoon. He and Dipper, with the small young man at the wheel, were driving across the desert.

"Another couple miles," said the giant, who had a large ordnance map spread out on his knees.

"We really ought," said his friend, "to let the authorities handle this business."

"Handle? All they want to do, those birds, is sweep the whole thing under the carpet. I want to know who and what killed Ralph."

"He's dead," said Dipper. "He's going to stay dead, no matter what you find out."

"Maybe I'm a lot simpler than you, Dipper,"

40

Smitty told him. "When somebody kills a buddy of mine, I go after that somebody."

Dipper didn't say anything for a moment. "Look, Smitty, don't get the idea I don't care about what happened to Ralph," he said finally. "The thing is, we're bucking some very important people."

"Early? What's so important about him? He's only a cop with some hush-hush Washington agency."

"But I work for the government myself, Smitty," Dipper reminded him. "If I keep on—"

"Okay," said the giant impatiently. "I won't drag you along on any more of my wild-goose chases. Maybe you ought to go back home, make like you was never here."

"No, I'll stick a while longer."

The bright hot desert shimmered all around them. Today there was no wind, only dry flickering heat.

"Taking a look at the place where Ralph stopped his car probably won't . . . Holy smoke!"

"What is it?" asked Dipper, automatically slowing their car.

"Must be a mirage," said Smitty. "I think I see a blonde in a polka-dot bathing suit standing up there beside the road."

"Where? Oh, yeah, I see her, too."

"Well, if this ain't an example of mass hysteria, we better stop."

"It's probably only an example of an overheated radiator," said Dipper. "There's her car off by the side of the road."

"Yeah, and spouting steam like Old Faithful."

The blonde in the polka-dot swimsuit waved

41

hopefully as their car slowed to a stop. "I'm afraid I'm not used to driving in this kind of country," she said, pointing at the steaming hood.

"Common occurrence in these parts, miss," said Dipper. "I'll take a look, but I think the best thing to do is going to be to let the car sit for a spell."

"I don't know," said Jennifer. "I don't really know much about machines."

The two men alighted. Dipper gingerly lifted the hood. While he squinted at the radiator and engine block, Smitty said, "My name's Smitty, and he's Charles Willet."

"Better known as Dipper."

"I'm happy you came along," said the girl. "my name is Jennifer Hamblin."

Dipper turned his head away from the engine. "Had a visiting prof named Hamblin once in my college days."

"At Cal Tech? It was probably my uncle, then."

"Val Hamblin," said Dipper, "a very smart guy."

"Yes, that's Uncle Val." She lowered her head and kicked at the sand. "That's why, in a way, I'm out here."

"I've heard of this Val Hamblin guy, too," said the giant. "If he's staying in these parts, I'd like to meet him."

"That's just it," Jennifer said. "I don't know where he is. I came out to southern California hoping . . . well, it's a long, dull story, really."

Dipper shut the hood and wiped his hands on the side of his khaki trousers. "She'll run again. after a little rest."

"You in a hurry, miss?" Smitty asked her. "We could drop you somewhere."

"No, not actually. I've been driving around most of the day to see if . . . well, it may sound silly. To see if I could spot any of these things they call black chariots. Have you heard any—"

"Say that again, miss." Smitty took hold of her arm.

"I was asking if you'd heard of the black chariots. There was only one mention of them in the papers, and my calls to the local law haven't produced one bit of—"

"You're interested in these flying gizmos, too?" the big man asked her.

"Yes, I am." She'd been looking up into his face, a frown on hers, as he questioned her. "You . . . I've seen you . . . no, your picture someplace."

"Smitty's somewhat of a celebrity," said Dipper. "You must have heard of Justice, Inc."

"Of course, that's why you seemed familiar to me," said Jennifer. She glanced at Dipper, then back at the giant. "There's something I'd like to talk to you about, Mr. Smith."

Smitty said, "You can say whatever you like in front of Dipper."

Dipper pointed at the blazing sun. "We should be able to find a cooler spot," he said. "I noticed a last-chance sort of cafe a mile or two back. Why don't we adjourn there?"

"Okay," said Smitty.

They called the little one Moron. The reason for that was . . .

He came in, adjusting his high-drape slacks, and crossed the windowless gray room. "Hey, did

43

you hear about the little moron who took the ladder to the party because—"

"Shut up, Moron," suggested the fat man in the chocolate-colored suit. His complexion was the same shade of gray as the walls.

"The trouble with you, Heinz, is you ain't hep." Moron dropped, with a clank, into one of the six metal folding chairs that made up the room's only furniture.

"You're fifteen minutes late," pointed out the third man in the room. His name was Trumbull, and he looked like hundreds of other tired middle-aged men.

"I drove over to the Springs," explained Moron. "I'm hunting for a Coleman Hawkins record that—"

"All right, enough," said the fat Heinz.

"I picked up a good one from the guy who runs the disk shop," said Moron. "Did you hear about the little moron who took the tape measure to bed because he—"

"They're not happy," said Heinz. The small folding chair was too small for his bulk; he kept shifting his weight uncomfortably. "We have to do better."

"I'd like to meet these guys," said Moron. "Who the hell do they—"

"They're the people we work for," said Trumbull. "They have a right to expect results."

"Yeah, well, I don't like being treated like a stooge," said the little man. "Never see these birds, get orders handed down to me by you guys. It lacks—"

"I've never seen them, either," said Trumbull. He took the display handkerchief from the pocket of his double-breasted blue suit and wiped his

44

forehead. "They pay well, and on time. That's all that need concern you."

Sighing unhappily, Heinz jiggled up off his chair. "They may not continue to pay us," he said. "They feel the last job was botched, very badly botched."

"We almost got that big stoop," said Moron. "We run him off the road good. It was just dumb luck that—"

"And dumb luck that he retaliated with some very unconventional weapons," said Trumbull, "is that what you really think, Moron? Dumb luck that he caught Rudy?"

"So he caught him," said Moron. "I notice Rudy ain't doing no talking. That stray shot of yours, Heinz, that was lucky because it kept—"

"The shot wasn't stray," corrected the fat man in the chocolate-brown suit. "They don't want any of us to fall into the hands of the opposition. I was merely acting on orders. Fortunately that pall of strange blackness was—"

"Hold your horses," said Moron, bouncing out of his chair. "You mean to stand there with your face hanging out and tell me you iced Rudy on purpose?"

"Exactly," replied Heinz. "Keep that in mind, Moron."

The little man sat down again. "Cripes," he muttered.

"Let's get on to new business," said Heinz, waddling slowly around the room. "They're giving us another chance to eliminate this man Smith."

"That's generous of them," said Moron, in a small voice.

Trumbull wiped his face again. "I've been

45

doing some quiet digging," he said. "It's as we suspected. Smith *is* part of the Justice, Inc., organization. Meaning there's a possibility more of his associates will be showing up."

"One or a bunch, we can handle 'em," said Moron. "What about that blond dame?"

"They have something else in mind for Miss Hamblin," said Heinz. "We are to concentrate on taking care of Smith, and any of his associates who appear on the scene."

"No sweat," said Moron, whose confidence was returning. "We can take care of a dozen like that big ginzo."

"With the proper plan," said Heinz.

CHAPTER IX

The Wrong Door

She saw him at twilight.

Jennifer was at the window of her second-floor room, idly watching the resort swimming pool below. A sun-baked old man climbed up the ladder at the shallow end, shivered into a white robe, and went paddling off across the sea-blue tiles. The entire pool area was empty now, the dozen round white tables unoccupied.

The girl was thinking about the conversation she'd just had with Smitty. "Justice, Inc.," she said to herself. "They might be able to help me. Yes, especially the Avenger. I've heard—"

Then she saw her uncle.

He came walking down a pathway lined with palm trees. He walked along the side of the pool, with that loping gait of his.

"Uncle Val!" she cried.

The tall, tanned man did not turn, didn't look up when she hailed him from her open window.

Jennifer leaned further out, calling again. "Uncle Val, up here!"

He passed the pool and turned down another pathway. This led toward the large building that housed the Oasis restaurant and ballroom.

The girl spun away from the window and ran across her room.

She ran down the empty corridor and hurried down the stairway. The first door she came to was marked Emergency Exit Only. She pushed through, out into the gathering dark.

"Uncle Val!"

He heeded her not at all. He went through a white door in the large building across the way.

Jennifer ran, with one fisted hand pressed against her throat. Pebbles of the white gravel flew up as she passed.

By the pool, then along the pathway. Into the other building.

There he was, turning down into that cross corridor.

"Uncle Val, don't you hear me? Why don't you wait for me?"

The long white hallway was quiet. Her heels seemed to set up an enormous clacking as she ran.

When she reached the next corridor, there was no sign of him.

The girl hesitated, staring ahead. Then she caught a flicker of movement.

"That next-to-the-last door on the left. It's just closing."

She began to run again.

This corridor, too, was empty. When Jennifer reached the door she'd seen easing shut, she stopped to catch her breath. She was positive the man she'd been following was her missing uncle. Why, then, hadn't he paid her any attention at all?

"Even if it's not Uncle Val, and I know it is," she said to herself, "I don't see why he didn't stop. He must be aware of my following him."

She took hold of the doorknob. "I know this is the right door." The door opened toward her.

The hall beyond was different. Not white like all the others, but a dim gray. Not much light, either, only a few small-watt bulbs in infrequent sockets along its length.

Taking another deep breath, Jennifer stepped across the threshold. The door closed silently behind her.

"Uncle Val," she said aloud.

Only silence.

She moved ahead, but more slowly. There were no other doors, nothing but the blank gray walls.

At the end of the hall she came to another door. She opened it. A stairway, leading down.

Even less light down there, only that one small bulb way off there. Jennifer's stubbornness took hold now. She'd come this far. She knew that was Uncle Val she'd seen.

She started down the wooden steps.

And after the next corridor there was another stairway. After that a winding, very narrow, passageway. All gray, dimly lit, and silent.

"Jenny, old girl," she said to herself, "this is all getting very strange. Maybe you ought to head for fresh air. Wait until the Avenger arrives, and tell him about this."

She turned back and went around the gray

passage. The door she'd entered by would not open now. Jennifer turned the knob again and again, and rattled the door. It would not open.

"Well, that pretty much decides my direction," she told herself. "Downward, ever downward."

She retraced her steps and came again to the end of the winding passage way. This door opened.

And there was Uncle Val, standing against the far wall.

"Uncle Val!" she said, starting toward him.

The three other men in the room did not let her reach him.

CHAPTER X

The Avenger on the Scene

The highway exploded.

Straight across its entire width. Great chunks of paving spewed up into the air, swirls of dust and smoke.

"Whoosh!" MacMurdie gave the steering wheel a violent twist. The nose of their car was not more than ten feet from the explosion.

Rock and asphalt pounded down on the machine as it went zigzagging toward the edge of the road.

"Up the boulder over there," warned Smitty, who occupied the seat next to Mac. "I spotted somebody."

"Get us behind that other spill of boulders," ordered the Avenger from the back seat.

Mac guided the bucking auto across the gritty

desert, dodging giant cactuses. "Do ye think we're in the midst of a Western-style ambush?"

"It's some kind of ambush, sure as hell," said the giant.

"By the Sacred Waters of Loch MacQuarrie!" exclaimed Mac while their car sluiced around a large joshua tree and then skidded to a stop behind a pile of dusty-orange boulders.

"Scatter!" Benson dived out the back door before the engine even died.

Smitty, tugging out an automatic, trotted into a cleft between two mammoth rocks.

Mac took up a position nearby. "Mot these be the same lads who tried to send ye off to the sweet by and by?"

"The survivors of that bunch, anyhow." Smitty ducked down.

An instant later, machine-gun slugs were zinging through the afternoon.

" 'Tis nae the most cordial welcome I've ever had."

Four members of the Justice, Inc., crime-fighting team had arrived in southern California an hour earlier. They had flown west in one of the Avenger's own planes, landing at a small private field. Smitty met them, and was driving the Avenger and MacMurdie into Manzana. Cole and Nellie, the little blonde none too pleased at the prospect, were heading together in another direction to book accommodations at one of the desert resorts.

Two, possibly three, men were fortressed in a mound of boulders some twenty yards to the south. The man with the tommy gun, like some lethal jack-in-the-box, would pop up, fire off a chattering burst, and then disappear.

Smitty glanced around the late afternoon desert. He didn't see the Avenger anywhere.

Another burst of machine-gun slugs spurted overhead.

The giant waited a second, stood up, fired two shots in the direction of the gunman, and dropped down again. Not with any expectation of hitting his man, but to provide a diversion. Benson was obviously up to something.

Silently, covered by the spills of afternoon shadow between the boulders, the Avenger was working his way toward their attackers.

He reached the bare stretch of ground between the two clusters of huge rocks. Three tall cactus trees grew across the empty space, about ten feet apart.

The machine gunner—it was the man we met as Moron—bobbed up once again to send another chain of slugs smashing toward what he believed to be the position of the three Justice, Inc., teammates.

Benson, unseen in the shadows, waited until Moron had hunched down out of sight again. Then he sprinted for the nearest tall cactus.

It was man-high, looking like an abstract sculpture constructed from prickly plumbing. The Avenger got to it undetected. He stood there, back against stickers, eyes narrow and watchful.

There were two other men with the gunner. He could see parts of them now as they crouched behind the boulders. A fat, profusely perspiring man clutching a .38 revolver, and a sad-faced middle-aged man with a rifle on the rocks before him.

The Avenger darted again, to the second cactus.

"Down there!" shouted fat Heinz. "I saw something, Moron. Quick!"

The Avenger's hand made a looping arc.

A pellet flashed through the bright air.

"Look out!" warned Trumbull, feet rasping on the stones as he tried to scurry back.

Too late. The pellet smashed, and blackness engulfed the three men.

The Avenger charged into the blackness.

"Would you care to change your guess and bet on twins?" asked Cole.

"You apparently," replied Nellie, "can make a joke about anything."

"That's not a joke, princess, it is merely a sporting proposition." He had an elbow resting on the open window of their rented car and was guiding the machine through the desert with one hand on the wheel. "But, yes, I imagine I could come up with a suitable quip for almost any occasion. Life, being noted for its unfortunate brevity, isn't worth being too sober-sided about."

"I'm not sober-sided," said the pretty little blonde, folding her arms. "I just think when one of our friends is having a baby you ought to—"

"This is very illuminating, Little Nell," grinned Cole. "You have a sentimental side, I never would have guessed."

"I don't have . . . Oh, nerts! There's no use arguing with you."

In the ensuing silence Cole commenced whistling a medley of the number one, two, and three songs from that week's Hit Parade list.

After a moment Nellie said, "Must you do that?"

"Would you rather I gathered grain for the hard winter ahead?"

Nellie took a deep breath and slapped her hands flat on her thighs. "I'm . . . not . . . going to . . . get angry with you," she said. "No, I am going to remain calm. After all, as you point out, life is short. Now and then fate throws one into the company of someone who is basically loathsome. The answer is, grin and bear it."

"That's the spirit, pixie. Learn to endure and . . . ah, there's a likely looking spot. The Oasis." He nodded at the resort that loomed up ahead of them.

"Looks expensive."

"You forget that I'm an executive, a tycoon, practically, and you're my highly efficient private secretary," said Cole. "We can afford the poshest of digs."

"If I'm so efficient, why didn't I make us advance reservations?"

"Haste. I'm the sort of tycoon who does things with head-spinning swiftness. There was no time to make advance reservations," Cole said. Making a lazy arm signal, he turned off the road and into the resort parking lot.

The attendant was talking to a waiter at the far side of the parking area. The waiter was a thin, gray-haired man, holding a round tray with two highballs on it.

Cole frowned. "Something deucedly familiar about the lad with the portable drinks." He turned off the engine.

"Hey, no!" called the attendant. He left his conversation to come running in their direction.

"Something amiss?" Cole eased out of the car.

"We're full up here at the Oasis, sir," the thickset attendant told him. "Sorry, this is our busy time. No use you parking. Sorry."

"Surely there's something," said Cole. "I'm Cole Wilson, III, of East Coast Aviation and I—"

"Nothing," said the attendant. "Sorry."

Cole was watching the waiter, who still stood at the far side of the parking lot. "Well, then, Miss Gray and I will have to try elsewhere," he said, climbing back behind the wheel.

"I'm sorry."

"So you said." Cole started the machine, backed out, and resumed the road.

"We picked too popular a place," said Nellie. "Why that scrunched-up expression on your face?"

"It signifies cogitation, my dear Watson," said Cole. "That waiter . . . I've encountered him somewhere before."

"So?"

"Not as a waiter, and not at a hotel or restaurant. It was someplace much more unsavory."

"You've probably been to a good many of those."

"Exactly, princess," said Cole, grinning. "Now I have to narrow it down."

CHAPTER XI

"It All Comes Back To Me Now!"

"Uncle Val," repeated Jennifer, "why . . .?"

A man held her right arm tightly; another stood at her left with a pistol pressed to her side. The third man, whom the girl recognized as the thin dark man who had appeared in the background when she checked into the Oasis, stood to one side watching her.

"Uncle Val, tell them to let me go."

Her uncle turned his back on her and left the room by way of a rear door. He said nothing.

"Now, then, Miss Hamblin," said the thin dark man.

Her eyes were still on the door her uncle had left by. "What's wrong with him? Why doesn't he—"

"What brought you here?"

"I . . . came to the desert to look for my uncle."

"To this particular place, to the Oasis. Why did you select this resort?"

"I didn't know Uncle Val was here, if that's what you mean," Jennifer said. "The travel agency I used in Boston told me it was . . . a nice place."

The thin, dark man watched her face for a full minute. "Perhaps," he said at last. "And why are you in southern California at all, Miss Hamblin?"

"I told you, to look for my uncle."

"The United States is a vast country. Why select this one particular area?"

"Because of the black chariots, obviously," she answered.

The man who was holding her arm relaxed his grip for a few seconds.

"You associate your uncle with those?" asked the thin dark man.

"He was working on something very similar before he . . . vanished," the girl said. "I assume you must know something about that, too."

"Yes, we do." He watched her, silent, for another minute. "It is most unfortunate for you, Miss Hamblin, that you have knowledge of the observation ships. I'm afraid you will have to stay with us for a while."

"As a prisoner."

"Let us say as a guest with some restrictions placed upon her."

"I don't see how you can keep me here," said Jennifer. "After all, people back in Boston know I'm out in California. The travel agency knows I was booked here."

"We can arrange things so that no one will miss you for quite some time, Miss Hamblin."

"Oh, really?"

"In fact, if it becomes necessary we can even arrange your . . . death."

Cole sat up on his still-made bed. "Eureka!" He tugged his shoes back on and hurried across the room and into the hall.

He and Nellie had taken adjoining rooms in a desert resort calling itself the Seven Dunes.

Cole knocked on the girl's door.

In a moment Nellie looked out. "Was that you bellowing next door?"

"Yes, pixie, I always tend to bellow when I have a momentous insight."

"You've had one?"

"I remembered who that waiter I spied at the Oasis is," he told her. "Let's get over there."

"Now?" It was after 10 P.M.

"The chap happens to be a suspected foreign agent," explained Cole. "I saw his mug in a collection of dossiers an FBI chum of mine let me peruse a couple months back. His name is Franz Bernhardt, age 59."

Nellie asked, "You're sure?"

Tapping his forefinger beneath his left eye, Cole said, "They don't call me Hawkeye for nothing. Of course I'm sure. Let's go."

Backing away from the door and collecting her purse, Nellie said, "You planning to walk right into the place and drop a net over Franz?"

"I don't have my entire strategy worked out. Right now, we can simply pop into the Oasis cocktail lounge and see how the land lies."

"They didn't give me the impression," she said

as she joined him in the corridor, "that they took too kindly to strangers."

"I'm not looking for acceptance and affection. I only want to have a little chat with Herr Bernhardt."

"Maybe the Oasis people don't know who he is." They started for the stairs. "But on the other hand, maybe they do."

CHAPTER XII

On The Trail

Earlier that day, at the tag end of the hot afternoon, the area sheriff was sitting in a wicker chair in front of his white-washed adobe Manzana office. He was attempting, once again, to roll his own cigarette.

"Now, darn!" muttered Sheriff Brown. "I ought to be able to do this. It would sure come in handy, too, what with ready-mades so hard to get. Darn." Half the tobacco slid out of the cigarette paper and down his sleeve.

A car came to a stop in front of the office. A huge man got out on the sidewalk side, wiped his forehead with the back of his fist, and said, "How you doing, sheriff?"

Brown, a chunky weatherbeaten man of fifty, stood up, spilling the rest of the tobacco out of his uncompleted smoke.

"Pretty fair, Mr. Smith. Help you any?"

Smitty held up a hand in a wait-a-minute gesture. "We got some bozos for you." He went around to the rear of the car, unlocked the trunk, and hauled out the unconscious Moron. Depositing him on the sidewalk, Smitty shut the trunk and moved to the back door of the car. From the back seat and floor he dragged two more unconscious men, Heinz and Trumbull. "These are the guys who tried to kill me the other day."

Flinging away the now empty cigarette paper, the sheriff hustled down to the curb. "How'd you happen to run across them?"

"They tried it again," explained Smitty.

Sheriff Brown noticed two men sitting in the front seat. He touched the brim of his cowboy-style hat. "Afternoon, gents," he said. "Would you mind coming inside and making some kind of statement?"

"Not at all," said Benson. He and Mac got out of the machine. "I'm Richard Henry Benson."

The name the sheriff recognized. He'd made a check on Smitty when the giant had brought in the dead ambusher. "Well, sir, the Avenger." He held out a hand. "Pleased to meet you."

"This is my associate, Fergus MacMurdie."

"Where shall I dump these guys, sheriff?" Smitty inquired.

"They're all alive, aren't they?"

"They've been rendered unconscious by an otherwise harmless gas," said Benson, not adding that the gas had also enabled him to question each of the men.

"Guess we better stick them into cells."

"Here, mon," Mac said to the giant, "I'll lend ye a hand."

"Take the little one," suggested Smitty as he picked up the other two, one under each arm.

The twilight thinned, and darkness began to drop down.

MacMurdie reached out and clicked on the floor lamp. A circle of light fell on the map Dick Benson had spread out on their room's coffee table. "A veritable castle, is it?"

"According to what Heinz was compelled to tell us," said the Avenger.

Smitty was roaming the hotel room, restless. "That Early guy is going to beat us to the punch," he said. "This here sheriff is going to fill him in on everything we told him. And with Agent Early's drag in Washington, he may be able to find out more about those bozos."

"No more than we learned when we used the truth gas," Benson assured him. "Anyway, we're not in a contest with Don Early."

"He thinks we are."

"I don't play by other people's rules."

Smitty shrugged. "Too bad those three clunks didn't know more."

"Only underlings they were," said MacMurdie.

"Heinz was the only one who had any contact with the people who employed his gang," said Benson.

"Aye, and even he has only a vague idea of what the skurlies are up to."

"It's obviously espionage of some kind," the Avenger said. "Heinz and company were used to handle simple jobs of dirty works. They're domestic crooks, for hire."

"They didn't even put in the first team against us," remarked Smitty.

"They will now," Mac assured him.

"How does all this link up with the chariots?" said Smitty. "Heinz didn't know much about them at all, and he had no idea who killed Ralph."

"Before we answer any more questions," said Benson, "we're going to have to do some more digging." He tapped the map. "Heinz got his instructions, and his pay, from this Old Man Guptill."

"That's kind of funny," said Smitty. "I heard about that guy, he's something of a local character—they got a lot of oddballs in these parts. Way I got the story, though, this Guptill coot has been holed up in his castle in the desert for years, since the Depression, just about. Seems funny he'd turn into a spy all of a sudden."

"Mot nae be all of a sudden," said Mac.

"Guptill may have been planted here years ago and told to wait," said Benson. "We've encountered other Axis agents of that sort, you'll recall."

"Sure, like that guy back in Connecticut that time," replied Smitty.

"There are several possible explanations for Guptill's part in all this." The Avenger stood up. "We'll look into that now."

CHAPTER XIII

Merger

"I don't mind surly waiters," remarked Cole Wilson, "but this is carrying it a bit far." He dodged as the red-coated waiter threw another punch at him.

The waiter, a low-foreheaded man with crinkly red hair, stumbled on by Cole, tripped over the foot Cole had placed in front of him, and whammed head-first into a table.

Glasses, a lit candle, and a copper ashtray were seesawed up into the chill air of the cocktail lounge.

The waiter fell, sprawled, and the highball glasses, shedding ice cubes, fell down on top of him. The candle missed him, extinguishing itself in the thick scarlet carpeting. The landing ashtray caught him square on the back of the skull.

"Another one coming," warned Nellie. "Two, in fact."

Two large men in dark suits were emerging

from a door behind the long bar. They said nothing, only grunted, as they galloped toward Cole.

"Gentlemen," said Cole with a grin, "I trust you'll be honorable enough to fight me one at a—oops!"

Both of them tackled him, one high and one low.

"Okay," sighed Nellie, "I might as well get in on this."

"Leave 'em be," cautioned the bartender, a bald man who now had a .32 revolver in his left hand.

"Oh, fudge," said the little blonde. She bent, as though to straighten a stocking. When she came up, very swiftly, a bar stool rose up, too.

Its tufted seat whumped into the bald bartender's chin. "Unk," he remarked as his teeth clacked tight together.

The pistol fell down behind the bar. So did the bartender.

Nellie rubbed her palms together and strode to the tangle that was Cole and his two assailants. Though she outwardly seemed to be a demure and defenseless, not to mention small, young lady, Nellie was far from it. She was, to put it simply, pretty tough.

She grabbed one of the dark-suited men by the neck, with her other hand gripping his wrist. The pressure on the big man's neck made him gag and let go of Cole. Using his arm as a handle, the little blonde flipped him across the cocktail lounge.

He landed on his tailbone, between two tables, but close enough to one to cause it to topple over sideways like a felled tree. It showered him with an ashtray, a candle, and a wooden bowl full of stale popcorn.

"Accept my," said Cole, delivering a jab to the remaining man's midsection, "grateful thanks, pixie."

"I'd do the same thing for most anyone."

"There." Cole connected with his opponent's chin; the man sagged and dropped to the floor. "Now what say we fold up our tents and get the—"

"Not quite yet, Mr. Wilson." A thin, dark man in a tuxedo was standing in the arched entryway to the Oasis lounge. A revolver in his hand pointed directly at Cole.

Nellie moved closer to Cole, nodding at the bar. "And another one back there with a gun, too."

"I'm starting to feel like General Custer on his farewell tour," said Cole. "You have the advantage, sir, in that you know my name and I don't know yours."

"My name is Danker, at the moment," said the thin, dark man.

"I see, Mr. Danker," said Cole. "Well, I am regretful that I felled several of your employees. Any number of the most fashionable members of café society will testify that I am usually very sedate when I visit nightclubs and similar bistros." He gestured with a thumb at the redhead waiter, who was now on his hands and knees and groaning. "However, when this chap suggested that I come along with him, I must admit I demurred."

"I'm afraid he was acting on my orders," said Danker. "You were recognized, Mr. Wilson, the moment you came in."

"I can see why you don't have much clientele," said Cole, "if you treat every familiar face this way."

"I truly enjoy badinage, Mr. Wilson. Let us, though, drop the banter for a moment." Danker snapped his fingers in the direction of the man behind the bar. "Search him, Dirks."

Dirks was large, too. His tuxedo, not quite as large as he was, strained at the shoulders and was taut as a sail in the wind across the back. He tilted to the left as he walked over to frisk Cole. "What about the broad?"

"That will be taken care of later."

"She's a pretty salty little skirt," said Dirks. "I saw what she done to Haefley. She threw him right on his—"

"Search the young man, Dirks," repeated Danker.

"I really don't see, old man, why you—" began Cole.

"I am familiar with the faces of all the members of the illustrious Justice, Inc.," said Danker.

"Ah, the price of fame," said Cole, lifting his arms.

Dirks began slapping down his sides. "Here's a rod," he announced, removing a pistol from its shoulder holster. "And . . . I ain't sure what this is. A handful of glass balls."

"You might drop one on the floor," suggested Cole. "That way you'll enjoy the full—"

"Hand those here, Dirks. Be careful."

Gingerly the big man let the half-dozen blackout pellets roll from his palm into Decker's. "Hot stuff, hugh?" He gave a massive shrug and returned to his search. "Here's some kind of screwy-looking knife. I seen a Chinaman use one once up in Frisco. It was back in—"

"You can spare me the narrative, Dirks." Danker took the knife and set it on a table.

"And what's this dingus? I remember a peeper planted something like this in my hotel room once when my second wife thought I was—"

"Let me have it." Danker took the small eavesdropping bug and placed it next to the confiscated knife. "You remind me of that motion-picture comic, one of the Marx Brothers, I believe, whose pockets contain a most amazing collection of devices and artifacts, Mr. Wilson."

"Probably because I'm something of a comedian myself."

"Yes, to be sure," said Danker. "Although I believe even you won't find much to be amused by during your stay with us."

"You can't hold us here," said Nellie. "If you know who we are, then you know we're part of a larger organization. They'll come looking for us, and that's going to mean only trouble for you."

"Forgive me for resorting to a cliché, Miss Gray, but the desert is a big place," said Danker. "It's quite easy for people to disappear in its sandy vastness."

"The Avenger knew we were going to pay this call on you, old man."

"Somehow, Mr. Wilson, I doubt that. Even if it were so, we are prepared to stand off an army here, if need be. And your much-touted Avenger is, if you'll forgive me for pointing it out, only one man."

"You're going, if *you'll* forgive *my* cliché," said Cole, "to be changing your tune very soon, Danker."

Dirks stepped back from him. "That's the lot. He ain't got nothing else on him."

"Very good. Now we'll have Helga search the young lady, after which we'll show them to their new home."

"Going to be guests of the Oasis, are we?" asked Cole.

"Yes, though you won't, I must apologize, have much of a view."

"Underground," said Cole, rubbing his neck below his ear. "Quite a way underground."

"This is the deepest-down basement I've ever been in," said Nellie.

Dirks and Danker had just shoved them into this windowless room and locked them in.

"Well, we. . . Hello, who's this? Another damsel in distress?"

Jennifer Hamblin had been dozing in a wooden chair in the shadowy corner of the room. She sat up awake now, blinking. "Who are you?"

Grinning at the pretty girl, Cole said, "I'm Cole Wilson, sometimes known as Devil-May-Care Wilson. This young lady is Nellie Gray."

Jennifer got up. "I've heard of you. In fact, your friend, Mr. Smith, was going to help me find my uncle."

"Ah, then we've heard of you, too. You must be Jennifer Hamblin."

She nodded, brushing her hair back from her face. "How did they get you? Was it because you were looking for me?"

"This is going to hurt my reputation for infallibility," said Cole, "but I didn't know you were missing. No, we breezed into the cocktail lounge an hour or so ago. I had, earlier in the day, spotted a chap named Franz Bernhardt gainfully employed here as a waiter. It was my original intent to case the joint, as it were."

"But," said Nellie, "they seemed to know who we were. Almost the minute we sat down, a punchy-looking waiter came over and tried to drag Cole off for an interview with this Danker guy."

"Danker?"

"Dark chap, with a lean and hungry look, very dapper."

"Oh, yes, him. He's the one who brought me here, but I didn't know his name."

Hands in pockets, Cole eased around the room. "Yon door would appear to be the only way out."

"Yes, I believe it is. Although you're probably much better than I am at finding your way out of places."

"Second only to Houdini and the great Norgil," Cole said.

"You mentioned a waiter named Bernhardt," said Jennifer, watching him pace the room. "Who is he?"

"FBI has the notion he might have ties with the Fatherland," said Cole. "Know him?"

She shook her head, sadly. "No, but it just confirms, more or less, what I've been thinking." Backing, she sat down again. "I've seen my uncle."

"Eh?" Cole stopped still.

"That's how I got here. I mean, I was up in my room, and I saw Uncle Val. He was outside, walking across the patio by the pool. I called and called, but he paid no attention. So I left my room and followed him. That led me down here."

"You're sure," asked Nellie, "it was him?"

Jennifer bit her lip, head downcast. Then she said, "Oh, yes, it's Uncle Val. I finally got as close to him as I am to you two. It's him, yes, for sure. He . . . I don't know . . . he was a . . . what do they call it? . . . A decoy, a stalking horse. He led me right into the trap."

Cole said, "What did the old boy have to say about it?"

"Nothing, he never spoke. He only stood by; then he went away, and Danker, if that's his name, had me brought in here."

"Why would your uncle be cooperating with these lads? It's beginning to smell as though we're in a nest of saboteurs and spies."

"Since you're here," said Jennifer, "you must have been told some of what I told Mr. Smith. My uncle, at the time he disappeared, was working on a disk-like information-gathering craft. A ship that could fly in low, virtually undetected by any existing equipment, and obtain photos of anything from a gun installation to a war plant. The ship was extremely maneuverable and compact. It would carry a single man, or could be radio-controlled. The government—our government, I mean—was very interested. And then Uncle Val disappeared."

"So you think your uncle built these black chariots that have been awing the locals?"

"When I read the single account in the paper, I thought of Uncle Val at once," said Jennifer. "You know the rest, I imagine."

Nellie said, "You're pretty certain he's working with these fellows of his own free will."

"What else can I think?"

Cole was watching the ceiling. "I don't detect

any listening devices, but one can never be sure," he said. "I think I'd better make our call right now, pixie."

"Yes, do."

"Call?" said Jennifer.

"When the heavy-handed minions of Danker frisked us," explained Cole, "they fortunately neglected to find the two-way radio I carry in my belt. If you'll excuse me." He unbuttoned his jacket, and then undid his belt.

CHAPTER XIV

Conversations

"Did you hear about the little moron who shot his father and mother so he—"

"Can it," said Heinz. He and Moron were sharing a cell in the Manzana jail.

"Only merely trying to keep up morale," said the little man. "Humor is a very important tool when—"

"Yes, yes, enough." The fat man was sitting on his cot, head held in both hands.

"Still trying to remember, huh?"

Heinz said, "I know he used something on us."

"Okay, but maybe it was only to knock us out."

"The Avenger is trickier than that," said the fat man. "No, I'm relatively certain he used something to make us talk."

"I don't remember nothing like that, Heinz."

"You probably don't even remember what you had for breakfast, so it hardly——"

"A bowl of Kellogg's Pep, coffee, and a maple bar."

Heinz, swatting the air with his hand, said, "Stop interrupting me, Moron. I . . . yes, I have the distinct impression of telling the Avenger things."

The smaller man shrugged his left shoulder. "So what? It ain't like you knew much."

"I know a good deal more than either you or that nonentity Trumbull," Heinz told him. "I know who hired me, who I was reporting to and getting orders from. It seems . . . I have the feeling I told him about that."

"I keep wondering who the brains was. Who was it?"

"No, there's no need for you to know."

"What's the diff now, Heinz? We're both in the pokey, not likely to go breezing out until the duration plus six. So confide a little, huh?"

"If I did tell the Avenger, it was against my will. That's the only way I'd betray a confidence."

"The way you talk, it's like we ain't in the same business, you know." Moron leaned against the adobe wall of their cell. "Okay, suppose you did tell this Avenger guy who the head cheese is . . . Is that so bad?"

"The people we've been working for, Moron, it isn't wise to doublecross them," said the fat man. "Although the man I dealt with was not actually the leader, he was rather a go-between."

"Then it maybe don't matter if the Avenger and his stooges grab the guy."

Heinz sat up. "It occurs to me, Moron, that by

75

now our employers will surely know of our capture."

"Sure, bad news travels fast."

Nodding to himself, the fat man continued, "And, being quite efficient, they'll probably operate on the premise that I did talk." He chuckled, nodding more. "Yes, that would be very nice."

"What would?"

"The surprise the Avenger is going to get."

Dipper Willet eased the hotel room door open. He scrutinized the hallway in all directions, then slipped out and walked rapidly to the back stairs.

Emerging in a night alley behind the hotel, Dipper hurried along it. A shaggy mutt dog was sleeping at its street end, but he only mumbled as Dipper passed.

In five minutes Dipper reached the small Mexican restaurant on one of Manzana's rundown back streets. The place was dark, a tattered shade pulled down over the glass door. A plaster bull, about the size of that sleeping dog, was hanging on a chain up over the entrance.

Dipper took hold of the doorknob and turned it. The door swung silently inward. He crossed into the dark little café. There were four small booths along the righthand wall. The young man sat down in the third from the door.

"Something to eat?" asked Don Early, who was seated across the table from him.

"I don't care much for Mexican chow."

"No, this is a box of sandwiches I bought at a lunch counter uptown."

"Thanks, no."

"Job like mine, you never know when you're

going to eat," said the government agent. "Well?"

"Smitty was back a while ago, very briefly," said Dipper. "His friend, Benson, and most of the rest of the Justice, Inc., gang arrived today. You knew that, didn't you?"

"Richard Henry Benson, Fergus MacMurdie, Nellie Gray, and Cole Wilson, yes. I knew."

"Seems like the opposition knew, too. They tried to blow up Smitty's car, which resulted in—"

"Know about that. Talked to Sheriff Brown a couple hours ago, running a check on those guys."

"Smitty seems to think they're only hired hands."

"So do I," said Early, reaching into the white box in front of him and taking out half a sandwich. "Where's your friend now?"

Dipper shifted on his bench. "I wish you wouldn't remind me that Smitty's a good friend of mine. I feel like . . . some kind of Judas, talking to you."

After taking a bite of his sandwich, Early said, "I'm not trying to entrap Smith, you know. We're on the same side, far as I know. It's just that . . . well, I'd like to solve at least one of these damn cases by myself. This one I really thought I could. Sure, I knew about Smitty coming West, but I was certain he didn't know anything about the Stonebridge Project."

"I don't think he does, even now, Early."

"Maybe not." He ate the sandwich for a while, chewing thoughtfully. "Look, Willet, there's no need for you to feel bad. You're working on a top secret project for the government yourself. And you know how important the Stonebridge setup

77

is. What they're working on there . . . well, it might help us win the war years sooner. Think of the lives that—"

"You really must feel guilty, Early. I've never heard you go in for pep talks before," said Willet in the dark. "Next thing I know you'll bring in Kate Smith to sing 'God Bless America.'"

"You're too cynical, Willet."

"If I was, I wouldn't have agreed to keep you informed on the activities of Justice, Inc. I think the Stonebridge Project is important, too. It's just that I hate to . . . well, forget it."

Early brought the remains of the sandwich half up near his eyes. "I ordered meat loaf and one egg salad. This isn't either." Shaking his head, he asked, "Where's Smith now?"

"Following up a lead."

"Okay, but where?"

"I don't know, out in the desert someplace."

"Didn't he say?"

"Nope, he came in to change clothes."

"What'd he put on?"

"I didn't pay much attention. Not a dress suit, if that's what you mean. Dark clothes, I think. A black pullover and dark slacks."

"Going to sneak up on somebody, maybe."

"I don't know."

Early said, "When he comes back, try to find out where he went. Okay?"

Willet sat in the darkness for a moment, quiet. At last he said, "Okay."

CHAPTER XV

Castle In The Desert

Smitty inserted two huge fingers under the collar of his dark turtleneck sweater and blew out his breath over his upper lip. "Pitch dark," he observed, nodding in the direction of the desert castle of Old Man Guptill.

"The old gent must be ta home," said Mac-Murdie, who was crouched beside Smitty on the rocky hillside above the fenced-in castle grounds. " 'Twas my impression recluses nae did much traveling."

"It may be," said the Avenger, "that they're expecting a visit."

"From us guys?" asked Smitty.

"From someone. By now they certainly know those three underlings are in custody." Benson pointed at the wire fence. "Take care of that, Smitty. Mac, you and I will go over the south side of the fence, down that way. Smitty, you come in from the north. We'll circle the place, come at the castle from the backside."

"Got you." The giant fished a pancake-size black disk out of his pants pocket. Bobbing his head up and down once, he left them.

Despite his bulk, Smitty could move quietly. He climbed down the steep hillside without disturbing so much as a pebble. Head hunched, he moved along the edge of the roadway.

"If they're in there," he said to himself, "we got maybe five minutes before they catch wise to what I'm going to do."

Smitty scanned the dark area beyond the fence. The sky was overcast tonight; there was no moon. He saw no sign of any guards.

Way off somewhere, a night bird made a fluting sound. Everything else was still.

"Too quiet," thought Smitty. "Like everybody was waiting for something to happen."

He slowed his pace as he drew nearer to the fence.

Only silence, darkness. No one else around, no one watching him.

He made an adjustment on the face of the disk he was carrying. Then, sucking one cheek in, he went running straight for the wire fence. He slammed the disk against the wire, with a pie-in-the-face shove. Then he pivoted and dropped back.

The fence made, for long seconds, a sizzling crackling sound.

"Well, she was electrified. And now, thanks to that little gadget, she's shorted out good."

The giant looked around him. Silence on all

sides. He began to trot parallel to the fence, heading north.

Mac and the Avenger reached the top of the fence at the same instant, let go, and dropped to the ground.

"Ma bones dinna feel quite right, Richard," said the Scot as they began cutting across the sandy acres. "Perhaps I'm jaded, but I'm suspicious of things what are too easy."

"It's possible the castle has been abandoned."

The castle rose up a quarter of a mile to their right, a vast deep black shape against the black night. There was not one light showing on this side of the castle, either.

Large cactus trees grew in jagged rows across the ground the Avenger and Mac were covering. It made the area look like a surrealistic cemetery.

"Whoosh!" exclaimed Mac suddenly. "There's . . . no, I was mistaken."

"See something?"

"'Tis not but one of those skurlie cactuses. I thought I saw one of its arms swing around with a gun in it."

They were now about a hundred yards from the side of the castle.

Benson stopped, looking up at it.

Mac halted, too. "There's nae a soul inside there," he said, shaking his head.

"I don't think so . . . and yet."

MacMurdie laughed quietly. "Wha's the matter wi' us, Richard? We're letting this pile of masonry spook us."

Benson resumed his approach of Old Man

Guptill's castle. His eyes glowed in that peculiar way they did at times.

When they neared the rear of the place, Mac said, "There comes Smitty, from over thata way."

The giant was moving stealthily toward the back of the silent castle. His big feet touched the stones of a pathway that twisted toward a rear staircase. High cactus and joshua trees lined the path. Smitty could approach quite close to the castle and still stay in the shelter of the trees and their shadows.

"I do believe the lad's going to walk right in."

"Smitty knows better, he'll wait outside."

They saw the big man take three more steps forward. Then he was hidden from them by a huge cactus.

An instant later, there was a tremendous explosion on the path. Orange fire erupted up into the black of the night as shattered rock spun away.

"Smitty," said Mac, starting to run.

CHAPTER XVI

Message Sent . . .

The walls were filled with large oil paintings, fairly good copies of 19th-century Impressionist works. With a glass of brandy in his hand, Danker seated himself in a velvet chair. "I would like to see Dr. Hamblin," he said.

The other man in the large underground room was young, a very fair blond in a very tight white suit. "I'll fetch him for you, Herr Danker."

"Stop using those old-country words, Kurt."

Kurt blushed. "I thought, Herr . . . I mean, when we are alone, I thought—"

"There is absolutely no need for you to think, Kurt," Danker told him. "Follow orders well, that's all you must worry about."

"Yes, Herr . . . yes, sir." He clicked his heels and bowed out of the room.

"Idiots," murmured Danker as he sniffed and

then sipped his brandy. "A mission so important, and they burden me, for the most part, with idiots. Oh, and those fools I hired, my auxilliary troops. Captured by the Avenger, dragged to jail. It's a wonder . . . Ah, good evening, Dr. Hamblin."

Jennifer's uncle gave equal emphasis to each word. "Good . . . evening . . . Mr. . . . Danker."

"Sit down opposite me, Doctor, if you will."

"Yes . . . I . . . will."

"You may leave us, Kurt."

"Very good, Herr . . . sir." The heels clicked together once more, and the blond young man was gone.

"Now tell me, Dr. Hamblin, how are you feeling?"

"I . . . am . . . fine."

"It gratifies me to hear that," said the thin, dark Danker. "Frankly, and I'm sure you, as a man of science, will appreciate this, the drugs we are using to control you are quite new and, therefore, have not been as thoroughly tested as one might hope for. Well, this war . . . we must sometimes cut corners."

"I . . . am . . . fine."

"Very good. Did you recognize that girl this afternoon, Doctor?"

"She . . . is . . . my . . . niece."

"Yes, exactly. It does not bother you to see her here, to know she is our prisoner?"

"It . . . does . . . not . . . bother . . . me."

"I am most glad to hear that." Danker set his brandy glass on an end table, rose up, and walked to a white cabinet that stood beneath an imitation Renoir. "Well, then, Doctor, if you will oblige me by rolling up your sleeve, I will give you your evening injection and then you—"

"Herr Danker, come at once!" Kurt had burst back into the room. "Herr Dirks wishes it!"

Leaving the cabinet open, Danker crossed to the doorway. "What is it?"

"A radio, the prisoners have a sending set," said Kurt, breathing through his mouth. "Herr Dirks just noticed it when he looked through the spy hole to—"

"Fools, I have none but fools on my staff!" cried Danker. "Remain here with Dr. Hamblin." He ran down the corridor.

"Do you hear me, Richard? This is Cole. They've got us underneath the Manzana Oasis. Some kind of bomb shelter sort of set up. Richard, are you there?"

Only silence came out of the belt-buckle radio.

"Repeating the message, Richard. This is Cole. Nellie and I and Jennifer Hamblin are being held under the Oasis. I suggest—"

"Please, drop that," ordered Dirks.

"This? Come now, Dirks, I was merely amusing the young ladies with a little parlor magic," said Cole, grinning at the approaching man. "You know, old man, pretending this is a radio. I was talking about how we were locked up under the Manzana Oasis in a—"

"Enough, that's enough." Angrily, Dirks swung out his pistol to knock the buckle and belt from Cole's hand.

As the man lunged, Cole stepped to the right, thrusting his leg between Dirks's. "Watch your step, old fellow."

"You—"

Dirks fell.

Nellie leaped.

"Atta girl, pixie!"

The little blonde had hold of Dirks's gun hand and was twisting the weapon from his grip. She came up with it in her own hand. "Stay right down there, buster."

Cole dropped down next to the fallen man. "Hands behind you, Dirks. Come on, come on, let's not tarry."

"You can't get out from here," warned the prone man. "We have many men, they will cut you down."

"All I need is your thumbs," said Cole, ignoring the threat. He undid one of Dirks's shoestrings and used it to tie his two thumbs tightly together. "Now, we'll utilize the other shoestring to tie your ankles. This is an old woodsman's trick I learned from a Dan Beard handbook my maiden aunt in Grosse Pointe once gave me."

"Let's get going, Cole," suggested Nellie.

Cole hopped to his feet. "Ready when you are. We have only to gather Miss Hamblin into the fold and . . . oh."

Jennifer was standing in the doorway. Immediately behind her, with one hand around her throat and a gun pointed at her temple, was Danker.

"You're very resourceful, Mr. Wilson."

"As I was telling your sidekick there, I used to be a Boy Scout."

"Your activities have caused me to change my plans," said Danker. "Since there is a possibility your message reached its intended recipient, you must all be moved from here at once."

"Could I have a room with a southern exposure next time?" asked Cole.

"You will enjoy your new quarters, Mr. Wilson," promised Danker. "As well, I am more than certain, as the means by which you are conveyed there."

CHAPTER XVII

. . . Message Received

The Avenger had caught up with the running MacMurdie and held him back with a restraining hand. "Not so fast, Mac."

"Smitty's nae doubt hurt, mon!"

"If he is, there might be another trap for us."

"Damn," complained a voice up ahead in the darkness. "I got cactus needles all over my hind end."

"Smitty!" said Mac.

They saw him now. "Gee, I hope I didn't give you guys too much of a scare," said the giant as they approached him.

"Hoot, I expected to find ye resembling a great large jigsaw puzzle."

"I thought I spotted a trip wire across the pass while I was sneaking up on the joint," explained Smitty. "So I tossed a hunk of cactus at the wire. Darned if my surmise wasn't right. Some fireworks, huh?"

"Aye, most impressive. And ye're nae hurt?"

"Concussion from the blowup tossed me a little farther than I expected," said Smitty, looking back over his shoulder. "Knocked me backside foremost into one of them prickly trees."

The Avenger had been watching the silent castle. "No one has emerged to see what his booby trap did," he said.

"I think, Dick," said the giant, "they all skipped."

"Probably so, but they quite probably left other traps behind. We'll proceed with caution."

The three men, alert and watchful, moved along the remainder of the flagstone path.

When they were quite near the stone stairway that led to the rear entry door, Benson halted once more. "I think there's another small surprise waiting at the top of those stairs."

Squinting, Mac said, "Aye, mot be another wire."

"We can use the Smitty method of defusing," suggested the giant as he reached up and, gingerly, broke off the arm of a cactus.

The Avenger said, "Okay, go ahead, Smitty." He and Mac backed away and flattened out on the ground.

Smitty, adding a baseball-pitcher windup to the procedure, threw the cactus and then ran.

It was a second before the cactus hit the trip wire that the two-way radio in the Avenger's belt buckle signaled that someone was trying to contact him.

Then there was a huge explosion. It shook the castle and the ground around it. The stone stairs, in great broken chunks, went spinning up into the air, and a whole section of brick wall came tumbling down. Smoke and dust rolled over the three of them.

Seconds went by. There were no further explosions.

"Geeze, they get bigger and better," remarked Smitty, getting to his knees. "If there's one more, it's going to be a beaut."

Benson, standing up, clicked on the radio receiver. "Quiet a minute, Smitty."

". . . pretending this is a radio. I was talking about how we were locked up under the Manzana Oasis in a—" came Cole's voice.

That was all. The Avenger tried to contact Cole, but could not.

"Sounds like he's in some kind of pickle," observed Smitty. "I wonder what interrupted him."

"We'll find that out," said Benson. "But I want to check this castle out first. Smitty, you and Mac get over to the Oasis right now."

"How you going to travel?" asked the giant.

"Don't worry about that," said Benson. "Get going. I'll go through this setup and join you there later."

"The lad said 'we,' " mentioned MacMurdie. "Which mot mean Nellie's in the soup with him."

"Yeah, we better get rolling." Smitty turned away and began walking for a way out of the grounds. "That Jennifer Hamblin dame was staying there, too."

"We'll see ye soon, Richard." Mac followed the giant.

The Avenger encountered no further traps. In

the basement of the castle he found the real Old Man Guptill.

The old man was slumped on a dirty cot in a stone-walled storeroom. The room's wooden door had been padlocked. "It's about time, dangburn it," muttered the old man as Benson let himself into the room. "I like my meals regular, you know."

"Who are you?"

"Well, who in blazes do you think I am, you sawed-off idiot? You locked me in here, didn't you?"

"No," said the Avenger. "I've come to let you out. Are you Mr. Guptill?"

"Dang right. I'm Old Man Guptill, the meanest and orneriest galoot in six counties." He tried to sit up, but fell back against the stone wall. "Leastwise I uster be. You boys ain't been feeding me right, that's it."

"How long have you been locked in here?"

"Seems like forever," said Old Man Guptill slowly. "Let's see . . . must be a couple months, at least. It was a dadburned surprise, I tell you that. My own guards turning on me. See, it's danged hard, what with the war, to get any kind of guards. So I kind of had to lower my standards. Dang, was that a mistake!"

"What can you tell me about the men who did this?"

"A bunch of goons they are," said the old man. "Big as heck, ugly as sin, all four of them. Now I used to, before this dangblasted war started, always have twelve guards at least. But now, I was lucky to get even four when the other bunch up and quit me."

"And you've been down here all the time?"

91

"Course I have. They didn't let me out for no vacations."

Benson put an arm around the old man's shoulders. "Then they've had someone impersonating you." He helped him to sit up.

"Impersonating me? You mean some galoot's been posing as Old Man Guptill?"

"Yes, and giving out orders to a gang of hoods."

"My treasure!" said Old Man Guptill. "That's what they must be after. I told them that from the first. It's my treasure you want, but I ain't never going to tell you where it is. And I never did, neither."

"Did they try to make you tell them?"

Scratching at his beard, the old man said, "Funny thing, mister. They never did. It don't make no sense."

"It makes sense if you realize they wanted to use your castle as a way station."

"Fer what? Who are these boys?"

"Foreign spies," the Avenger told him.

"Well, I'll be hogtied and dipped in sheepdip, if that don't beat all," said Old Man Guptill. "I didn't even know they had spies these days. I figured that all went by the board when we trounced Kaiser Bill back in '18."

The Avenger to the old man to his feet. "I'd better get you to a doctor."

"Not on your life, young feller. Old Man Guptill never leaves the vicinity of his treasure," the old man insisted. "Bring the doc to me."

"Do you have a car?"

"Nope, can't see the need of one. Long as a man's got a few good horses, he got no need for an automobile."

Benson almost smiled. "I'll borrow one of the horses, then."

"Welcome to it, if them goons didn't steal them all," he said. He suddenly took hold of Benson's arm. "Am I right in figuring they done took off?"

"Yes, I've been through the entire castle. There's no one else here."

Nodding, Old Man Guptill said "Well, sir, that's good to hear. Sure, you go around to the stables and pick out my best horse. You know how to ride, don't you?"

"I do," said the Avenger.

CHAPTER XVIII

A Chariot Ride

Footsteps echoed on the metal floor. The huge oval room was chill, smelled of oil and fuel. Metal ribs fretted the walls and the ceiling.

"Uncle Val's ships," said Jennifer in a low voice as they were ushered into the underground hangar.

There were six of the craft in this particular room, each resting on small, fragile-seeming landing gear.

"This is the first time you've seen one, eh, Miss Hamblin?" asked Danker.

The girl didn't answer.

"Though from what your uncle tells me, you were allowed to see his various working models."

Cole surveyed the row of disk-shaped craft. "How many miles to the gallon do you get?"

"Very droll, Mr. Wilson." Danker consulted

his pocket watch. "Soon the three of you will have the rare opportunity of riding in these air-ships."

Cole whistled a little of "Swing Low, Sweet Chariot."

"What," inquire Nellis, "is the exact purpose of these things?"

"That need not concern you, Miss Gray."

"Maybe they want to scare the natives," suggested Cole, "so they can lower the real estate values hereabouts."

"There must be something," said Jennifer, "something around here they want to spy on. That's what the ships are intended for."

"A defense plant or a government project, mayhap?" said Cole.

"Yes, I imagine it's something like that."

Cole frowned. "I have the impression the Army Air Corps boys wouldn't stand still for anything like that."

"These ships are designed to avoid any method of aircraft detection now in use in your country," said Danker. "Should they actually encounter one of your stodgy conventional planes, they can easily outfly it."

"No propellers," said Nellie.

"They work on a different principle," said Jennifer, "more like a rocket."

"As much as I would like to prolong this pleasant discussion," said Danker, "I must now begin getting you aboard your respective ships."

"You're breaking up the set?" asked Cole.

"Only one of you can fit in each cabin along with the pilot." He smiled at Cole. "You'll be happy to learn that you're traveling with Dirks."

"Yes, it's nice to meet an old friend on a trip."

95

"You'll also be securely bound," added Danker.

"But not that securely," Cole thought to himself.

The disk-craft was humming through the night, heading out over the desert.

Dirks sat hunched at the controls, muttering to himself now and again.

"If you'd like to stop somewhere for a bite to eat, it's all right with me, old man," Cole said aloud. He was sitting on the floor of the small cockpit, hands tied behind him.

"How much you make a year?" asked Dirks, not looking at him.

"My work isn't actually of a salaried nature."

"What I figured," said the big man. "I been around a lot, you know, and I never seen a smart-mouth guy yet who ever made big money. You know why that is? I will tell you. It's because nobody likes a smart-mouth guy."

"How about Fred Allen, Fibber McGee, Edgar Bergen, Joe Penner, Jack Pearl?" Cole had his right wrist halfway out of the restraining ropes.

"Joe Penner ain't on the radio no more."

"He passed on."

"See what I mean?"

They were flying low over the flat desert, not more than a few hundred feet up. Now the ship began wobbling slightly.

"Bumpy road?" said Cole.

"Wind," said Dirks. "Wind coming up. One thing this crate ain't no good in, it's wind. Course, I remember a crate I flew back in 1933. I had me a job with an air circus. I would come roaring over this field full of rubes in this checkerboard biplane. I'd jerk this special little knob I had rigged up, and colored smoke would start coming out the rear end. It was something."

Cole concentrated on working his hand further loose from the ropes. He said nothing.

After a moment Dirks asked, "Ain't you got no smart-mouth remark about that?"

"Some things are too beautiful for words."

"I maybe could have been somebody in that racket, the aviation dodge," said Dirks. "Somebody like Roscoe Turner. I might look pretty good with a little mustache like his. But my first loyalty is to my home country, so that's why I'm doing what I'm doing."

"It's just as well. A mustache wouldn't suit you at all." He had the hand free. The tangle of ropes fell away, and Cole could use both hands.

Dirks said, "That blonde, she's kind of cute."

"Which blonde?"

"The tall one, not the little one. Oh, I suppose the little one ain't bad, but I never took to small women. Once in Columbus when I was traveling with—"

Cole had gotten a half-nelson on the man. "Okay, Dirks, here's what you do, old fellow, if you don't want to choke before your time."

"Watch out, that's dangerous."

The chariot was wobbling more wildly now.

"Set this thing down, right now," ordered Cole.

"We ain't near nothing," protested Dirks, gasping for air. "It's no place down there."

Cole reached around and took the man's revolver from under his jacket. "I imagine if we sit here in the desert till sun up somebody will spot us."

"Look, let me set it down near a highway at least, huh?"

Pressing the gun to the back of Dirk's thick neck, Cole said, "Very well, chum, but no cuteness."

"I got a great fear about being lost in the desert. Ever since I seen *Beau Geste* the last time."

Cole glanced down through the window of the small cockpit. There were no lights below them at all. "How far do you have to fly to find us a touch of civilization?"

"Not far, pal, not more than fifty miles or so. This baby'll cover that in—" Dirks threw himself to the side, then swung back a fist.

He hit Cole in the Adam's apple. Cole gagged and stumbled back. He started to bring the gun up.

Dirks hit him again. "You ain't as smart as you think, pal."

Cole went to his knees, and his head banged against the back of the pilot seat.

"Now, we'll continue . . . Holy smokes!"

The craft was bobbing through the darkness, swooping down, spinning up.

"See what you made me—"

There was the ground. The craft met it.

CHAPTER XIX

Barging In

The bearded old man swung his lead-tipped cane in the direction of the registration desk.

The clerk flinched.

"Dadburn it," shouted the old man, "I want to see the goshdarn manager of this here pesthole."

The clerk was slowly sinking out of range, in case the cane whooshed again through the air. "That's quite impossible, sir. Mr. Danker is . . . otherwise occupied."

"Well sir," said the expertly disguised Avenger, "he better unoccupy himself. Otherwise I'm going to go right straight into Manzana and talk to about a half-dozen shyster lawyers."

Smitty, wearing now a dark suit and a chauffeur's cap, stepped up beside Benson. "Maybe you ain't aware of who you're chinning with, buddy. This is Old Man Guptill."

"But he's . . . that is, I really can't help you, Mr. . . . . Guptill, is it?"

Smitty reached a giant hand across the desk and caught one lapel of the clerk's dinner jacket. "Old Man Guptill is giving you bozos a break, a chance to settle out of court."

"Dangnab, I'm losing my patience." Benson pounded the mosaic flooring with his cane.

MacMurdie, who had been sitting in a chair and pretending to read a newspaper, arose now. He joined the group. "I couldna help overhearing, sir. Perhaps I mot help ye, being I'm an attorney."

"That's danged good news," bellowed the Avenger. "I want to sue this whole Oasis place for kidnapping me."

"Please, sir," pleaded the clerk, "keep your voice down."

"I'm going to hoot and holler till I get some satisfaction. I just done got loose, and I got me proof positive these galoots are the ones who done me dirt." He leaned an elbow on the counter. "All-fired mad as I am, I retain my cool business head. I'm willing to let the whole mess get shoved under the rug . . . for a substantial piece of hard cash."

"Dinna be too anxious," cautioned Mac. "From what I can tell, Mr. Guptill, ye've an iron-clad case against these berkies."

"Uh . . . you'd . . . yes, come along with me, Mr. Guptill." The clerk, warily, emerged from behind the protection of his desk. "I'll escort you to our other building, where the business offices are housed."

" 'Bout time, sonny boy."

The clerk, with many looks around, led the

trio out of the main building of the resort, down a gravel path, and alongside the deserted pool.

"Not much business going on," remarked Mac.

"It's the . . . off season," said the clerk.

"Funny, I heard," put in Smitty, "that you was full up to the brim with guests."

"Well, yes. But a good many of them are older people. They come out only at . . . ah, allow me to open the door." He held open the door that Jennifer had followed her uncle through. "If you'll wait over there in the ballroom, I'll see if I can find Mr. Danker and fetch him here."

"You better be mighty dang quick about it," Benson told him. "I feel a spell of impatience coming on agin."

There were no customers on the huge dance floor. A six-piece band, however, occupied the elevated bandstand at the far end of the dimly lit room. They were not performing. Four of them were playing poker, using one of the drums as a card table. The other two watched. They were all big men, broad-shouldered. At least three of them were in need of shaves.

"Boys," said the clerk from the threshold, "perhaps you could entertain these three gentlemen." He made several hand gestures in the air.

"Sure thing," said the one with the most stubble. He hopped from the low stand, jabbing a hand into his jacket pocket as he did.

"Pair of knucks," said Smitty. He rubbed his big hands together in anticipation. "I smell a fracas."

"What kind of shenannigans you got in mind, sonny?" Benson turned toward the clerk, but the man was already slipping away.

He slammed the ballroom door and locked it on them from the outside.

"By the grizzled beard of Hereward the Wake," said MacMurdie, dropping the newspaper he'd been carrying under his arm, "I do believe it's a donnybrook in the making."

Three more of the burly musicians left the stand and came shuffling across the polished floor.

The leader, fitting the pair of brass knuckles to his fist, said, "You guys trying to make trouble for this joint, huh?"

"You ain't seen half the trouble I can make, young feller."

"Skinnay," the leader said to the man on his left, who was as husky as the rest of them, "you take care of the old geezer, since you're just getting over a cold. He'll be easy."

"Yeah, their bones break real easy," said Skinnay with a pleased chuckle. He leaped for Benson.

Benson was not there, however, any more.

Skinnay hugged thin air. "Hey!"

The Avenger was to the left of him. He chopped down against Skinnay's thick neck with the side of his hand, hard, three times.

"Gah," said Skinnay. His entire body shivered; then his right knee bammed against the hard dance floor.

Another chop from the Avenger sent the man sprawling.

"That's a pretty spry old coot," observed one of the other hefty musicians.

The leader was too preoccupied to reply. He had taken a swing, with his brass knuckle fist, at Smitty.

The giant had caught his hand in his. He was squeezing now.

"Cripes," gritted the leader. "Let loose, will you?"

"Okay." With a final powerful crunch Smitty shoved the man away.

The brass knuckles were bent and twisted, cutting into the man's fingers. "Get these damn things off me, somebody."

Before any of the other four could move, Smitty grabbed one of them. "You guys could use a little more exercise," he said, clutching the man by the armpits and spinning him around. "Or maybe a little airplane trip." When he let go, the musician sailed across the room, landed on the bandstand, and knocked over the trap drum.

"Hout, here comes a gun," warned MacMurdie, diving for the impatient musician who'd decided fists weren't going to work.

The agile Scot got hold of the weapon while it was still half in the shoulder holster. Shoving it back, he simultaneously jabbed the gunman twice in the stomach.

"Woof," said this one before collapsing.

In the Avenger's hand now appeared the strange tubelike pistol he called Mike. He leveled it at the two untouched musicians. "I advise you to forget about overcoming us," he said in his cold, even voice.

"Sure, we got no quarrel with you folks," said one.

"All a misunderstanding," said the other.

The leader was grimacing. "Get these damn knuckle-dusters off me," he said.

"In a moment," said the Avenger. "First I want something from you."

"What, what?"

"Information," said the Avenger.

CHAPTER XX

Wind

Danker paced the stone floor. "Dirks was only moments behind us," he said. "And now, almost an hour has passed and he is not here." Crossing the large underground cavern, he mounted a metal ladder and climbed up to the jagged ceiling. Danker slid aside a metal panel and ascended another metal ladder.

This placed him in a small room cut out of the rock. He pushed a button set in the stone wall, and a section of the ceiling slid away. This revealed a tough plastic dome, which gave him a view of the night sky above.

"If there's been an accident," he said as he picked a pair of powerful binoculars from the floor, "we may have serious trouble."

A swirl of sand rasped against the outer surface of the observation dome.

Danker stopped with the binoculars halfway to his eyes. He looked instead at a series of dials and gauges set in the stone wall.

"Can that be right? The wind is blowing at the rate of eighty miles an hour." He bent and read the wind velocity dial again. "Yes, it is correct."

Straightening, the dark, thin man put the glasses to his eyes. He could see nothing out there now in the night, only the sand being carried on the howling wind.

"There is no way to search for that idiot now," he said, closing the roof of the dome. "No, the ships cannot fly in this."

Down below, the young blond Kurt smiled hopefully as Danker climbed down the ladder. "You have good news, Herr . . . that is, Mr. Danker, sir?"

"Idiot," Danker said. He realized he was still carrying the binoculars. Snorting, he flung them at the nearest wall of the cavern.

"Something terrible has happened, sir?" asked Kurt, his smile dropping from his face.

"Where's Cole?" asked Nellie. She and Jennifer, still tied, were against the wall with two armed men standing nearby.

"That, my dear Miss Gray, is a question I am not, unfortunately, able to answer."

"What do you mean? Isn't he coming here?"

Danker said, "He was supposed to, yes."

"Has there been . . . a crash?"

"All I know is that there is a very formidable sand storm in progress outside now," said Danker. "Dirks and your smirking associate were due to land within moments after we did. I do not know what has delayed them."

"If they crashed—" began Kurt, slapping his forehead.

"See that these two young ladies are made comfortable in the barracks area," said Danker. "I must make preparations for any eventuality." He left them.

Jennifer rubbed her wrist. "You're fond of him, aren't you?"

The two of them were locked in a narrow room with two bunks in it.

"Of whom? You mean Cole Wilson?" Nellie sat down on the edge of one of the bunks and dangled her feet.

"Yes, I was noticing the way you two act together and I—"

"We're part of a group, that's all," said Nellie quickly. "I'm equally fond of all the members in the Justice, Inc., team."

"Oh," said Jennifer. "Perhaps, being an outsider, I didn't see what I was supposed to. Do you think Cole may have been able to take the ship away from Dirks?"

"That's what I'm hoping," said Nellie. She left the bunk and began circling, slowly, the room that was their prison. "If there really is a sand storm up there, well, I don't know."

"He knows how to handle a plane, doesn't he?"

"Cole's an excellent pilot," said the little blonde. "Well, I mean, they all are. You have to be, to work with Dick Benson."

106

"What's he like, the Avenger?"

Nellie didn't immediately answer. "It's difficult to put into words," she said at last. "He's unlike anyone else I've ever met."

"He may have received that message Cole sent out," said Jennifer.

"Yes," said Nellie, "so we can probably count on somebody getting here eventually to spring us from this joint." She jabbed a fist into her palm. "I'd like, though, if you want the truth, to get us free and clear of here by myself."

"How?"

"That's the snag," admitted Nellie.

Everything was a dusty chill blue.

"Banshees," muttered Cole, managing to rub a hand over his face. "Is that banshees I hear howling out there?"

He opened his eyes further and took a deep breath.

"Come to think of it, I've never heard a banshee howl."

Something was keeping him from rising. Something heavy, a dead weight atop him.

"I say, Dirks, old fellow, what say you grab your socks and get off your ox, as we used to say around . . . Oh, Lord."

He realized that Dirks would never, of his own will, move again. The big man's skull had an impossible dent in it, smeared with blood and hair.

"Excuse the rude remarks, old man." Straining, Cole managed to roll the dead man off him.

Dirks thudded to the floor of the cockpit. His body was not yet stiff. It assumed a new, folded-in position.

Rubbing the side of his head, Cole said, "Well, now, let's get our bearings, Captain Nemo." He glanced up at the cockpit cover.

Everything looked very odd out there. And the howling went on, seeming to shake the fallen chariot with its intensity.

Cole checked his wristwatch. It said eleven, but didn't seem to be working any more.

"It seems to be morning out there," observed Cole, "which would indicate I was out all night." He shifted and worked himself up into the pilot seat. "Wonder if they put radios in these things? Nope, not a sign of one. And all the other instruments seem to be in worse shape than my watch." He fisted a bent compartment door until it fell open. "There seems to be a bit of rations in here." He took out a packet of crackers and a Thermos. He jiggled the bottle and got a gurgling response. "Something liquid, anyway."

The chariot gave a violent shudder and seemed to take a small hop across the ground.

"Ah, yes, Wilson, is your head sufficiently clear to take in what that is that's going on out there?" he said to himself. "Yes, sir, it seems to be a fullblown sand storm."

Sand and wind worried the cockpit, buffing at it.

"Sooner or later, someone's likely to spot this downed curiosity," Cole said. "Of course, it might be some Air Corps boys, and then again it might be Danker. So the question seems to be, do I stay here and wait, or do I leave my cocoon and brave the elements?"

Frowning, he unscrewed the lid of the Thermos.

CHAPTER XXI

The Night Before

Val Hamblin noticed his hands. They were folded in his lap. The professor moved them and gripped the arms of the blue chair he found himself sitting in.

It was very odd. He knew where he was, and yet he didn't. The here and now was somewhat blurry, not as vivid as the past—as the night they'd grabbed him on campus, in the grove of maples behind the faculty club.

By pressing down with his hands, Hamblin pushed up out of the chair.

That was a long time ago, when he was drugged and brought here. He realized that.

Weeks ago. No, wait. It was more like months. Yes, they'd kept him drugged, under their control for months here.

Until tonight.

Danker had rushed off, some emergency. No one had remembered to give Hamblin the injection that would keep him under their control. He'd been put in his room, as usual, but there had been no injection.

"Jennifer," said the professor now, remembering more. "She's here, too."

He realized that although the effects of the drugs were wearing off, he was still not completely himself.

"Got to get out of here," he told himself. "Get out and find Jenny."

The door of his room, he remembered, was never locked.

No need to lock it. They were sure of him, sure that Professor Val Hamblin was docile and obliging.

Until tonight.

He turned the doorknob and pulled the door slowly inward.

There was a man out there. A large man with a pistol casually thrust in his belt. "Something wrong, prof?"

Hamblin put his hands to his temples. "Yes . . . it's . . . you'd better come in to my room . . . at once."

"Huh? You having some kind of fit, or what?"

The professor backed away, picked a heavy bookend up off the case behind him, and held it out of sight of the approaching guard. "Something terrible . . . has happened . . . in here."

"What? What for cripes sake?"

"I'm myself again," said Hamblin as he brought the bookend down on the man's skull. "For you that's terrible, for all of you."

He was out in the now empty corridor before the guard finished collapsing on the floor.

MacMurdie replanted his feet and threw another punch.

"Ump," said the underground guard who caught the blow in his ribs.

Mac followed with two jabs to the wobbling man's jaw. "That should take care of ye, lad."

It did.

Mac was free to continue on his way. The Justice, Inc., trio had separated once they'd gotten down under the Oasis complex. Thus far the Scot had encountered three members of Danker's crew. Of Cole, Nellie, or the Hamblin girl he'd found not a trace.

" 'Tis some setup these Axis skurlies have built for theirselves doon here," he remarked to himself as he descended a ramp-like corridor.

There was another door at the ramp's end. MacMurdie stopped there, listening.

From behind him came the sound of a piece of the metal wall sliding aside.

"Who the blazes are you, causing all this havoc down here?"

Mac turned to see who had asked the question.

Stepping out of the wall was a bearded man with an automatic trained on the Scot.

The giant Smitty tugged open the door he had found. To step through it he had to walk over the unconscious gunman he'd just now deposited on the floor.

"Holy smokes!" he exclaimed. "The black chariots!"

There were another half-dozen of the craft in this second underground hangar.

Walking softly, as he might in a cathedral, Smitty made his way across the hangar floor.

He stopped in front of one of the ships, hands on hips, and studied it, with slightly open mouth.

Then his mouth clamped shut and took on a grim expression. "This must be what killed Ralph, one of these babies."

Curious, Smitty climbed up to the cockpit. He saw how to open it, and did so. "Yeah, pretty compact," he observed after squinting in at the control panel. "You got to hand it to that Doc Hamblin. He knows his apples, that's for sure."

Smitty hunched his shoulders very slightly. Someone else was in the vast room with him. He could sense it.

Val Hamblin came around a turn in the corridor and stopped still.

Up ahead one of Danker's men was stepping out of a door in the wall.

"But it's not me he wants," the professor realized.

No, the man was holding a gun on the sandy-haired man down there.

Hamblin had no idea who the intruder was, but he decided that any enemy of Danker's must be a friend of his. Very carefully he began to approach the back of the man with the automatic.

"Come on, come on," said the gunman to Mac, "who are you?"

The Scot turned around to face him. "The name is Fergus MacMurdie," he said. He kept his voice calm, even though he now saw Hamblin approaching.

112

The professor still held the bookend in his hand. "That name," he said to himself. "Mac-Murdie, I've heard that name somewhere before." It was no use, he couldn't place it. Time, he was going to need time to remember everything, to get control of his own mind back completely.

"How'd you get in here?" the gunman demanded of Mac.

"I kin see where ye mot be worried about that, mon," said Mac. "Ye'd best hand over that blunderbuss of yours. I'm only the first wave of the invasion."

"Huh?" said the man. And then, "Unh!"

Hamblin had struck him down. He watched the guard fall. "Very good," he said. "Good evening . . . it is evening, isn't it?"

"Aye, that it 'tis."

"I'm . . . Val Hamblin, Mr. MacMurdie."

"Hout!" said Mac. "Ye're one of the lads we're hunting for. Do ye know where they've got your niece, mon?"

The professor ran his tongue over his lips. "Uh . . . let me think . . . You'll have to excuse me, MacMurdie, until very recently I've been . . . drugged by them. I . . . I'm still not . . . but let me think," he said, letting the bookend fall to his side. "I saw her earlier . . . and I can take you there. Yes, I can take you there . . . Come along." He turned and began walking away.

MacMurdie followed.

"Easy, Smitty," said the Avenger.

The giant straightened up and dropped down to the hangar floor. "Hey, I'm getting pretty good if I can hear you sneaking up, Dick," he said, "I thought at first it might be more of them Nazis sneaking in here." He waved a huge hand at the chariot he'd been investigating. "This is them, the black chariots."

"I realized that," replied Benson. "Think you can fly one?"

"I can fly anything," answered Smitty. "But why, how come?"

"I've been asking, with the help of the truth gas, a few questions."

"Great, where's Nellie and Cole?"

Benson said, "Not here any longer, I'm afraid."

"Ah," said Smitty, his face falling. "Not the Hamblin dame, either?"

"No, all three of them have been taken to another concealed hangar setup," said the Avenger. "Out in the desert, in a much less settled section. There's a man named Danker in charge of this whole operation. He and several of his henchmen flew there an hour or so ago, using some of these aircraft of Dr. Hamblin's."

"Yeah, what about the doc? They haul him off, too?"

"He's being held here," said the Avenger. "After we—"

"Whoosh," called MacMurdie. "Ye kin nae guess who I have with me, Richard." He stepped out of a doorway in the hangar wall, followed by Hamblin.

"It looks like Val Hamblin," said Benson.

"Aye, it 'tis indeed. And he saved me from having a few .45 slugs added to my carcass."

"I've been . . . trying to find my niece. But she isn't where she was . . . I thought perhaps they'd brought her to one of these . . . hangars."

"They did," said the Avenger. "They've taken her, along with two of my associates, away."

"Away . . . What do we do now?"

"Go after them," said the Avenger.

CHAPTER XXII

The Morning After

Agent Early shifted his folded raincoat from one arm to the other. He made a low whistling sound, not evidencing pleasure. "Had a notion," he said to Sheriff Brown.

"Beg pardon?"

"Before I even got here." Early moved farther along the underground corridor. "Premonition, almost a vision. They'd beat me to it."

"You mean the Avenger and his gang?"

"Him, yes."

All along the corridor were sleeping men. They were Danker's henchmen. A harmless gas, concocted originally by MacMurdie, had put them all to sleep before the Avenger and his gang had taken off three hours ago.

Early, along with the sheriff and several other

agents and lawmen, had arrived almost two hours ago. He'd been alerted by Sheriff Brown, who'd had a call from Smitty.

The young government agent walked on by the unconscious spies and gunmen. He slowed and peered through an open doorway. "Here's another hangar," he said over his shoulder.

"Anything in it?"

"Couple airships," said Early, crossing the threshold. "Yeah, we've found the chariots."

"Sort of uncanny, ain't it? How that Avenger fellow always—"

"Talk about something else." Early walked up to one of the chariots that had been left behind. He bent, studying its underbelly. "Cameras. So they took pictures." He turned and went back to the doorway. "Reisberson," he called down the hallway, "look for film, cameras, a darkroom."

"Right, sir."

Sheriff Brown reached out and touched the ship. "I got an impression," he said to the returning Early, "I don't know everything that's going on in my area. What would these boys be taking photos of, anyhow?"

"Something we don't want anyone taking pictures of."

" 'Bout a year ago you government boys fenced off about ten square miles out in the middle of no place, out beyond Lucifer's Playground," said the sheriff, watching the cleancut young man. "That's where it is, ain't it? I mean, whatever it is."

Nodding, Early moved along to the other craft and inspected its underside, too. "You don't want to know any more about the thing, sheriff."

117

Brown shrugged. "Okay, if you say so."

"Tell me again," requested Early, "what Smith told you over the phone."

"Said as how he and his buddies had caught themselves a spy ring, under the Oasis here, of all places," said Sheriff Brown. "Told me to give you a buzz on the telephone and let you know. He figured as how you'd appreciate catching a whole flock of spies, and the black chariots as well. Then, of course, he mentioned as how they'd also rescued this Dr. Hamblin and how he'd been drugged and all. They was leaving him here for us to—"

"Yes, I know. I just spent twenty minutes talking to Hamblin. He's pretty vague about a lot of things yet."

"Well, if you'd been abducted and shot full of—"

"Okay, but about where they were going next?"

"Taking some of these screwy flying machines and going off to catch the rest of the spies, that's all he said."

Early sighed, giving off again the sad whistling sound. "Could be any place," he said. "Maybe I can question some of these guys they left behind."

"This afternoon."

"This afternoon? They aren't going to wake up until then, not a one of them?"

"Smith said the stuff they used on them, whatever it might be, would keep them out for near a day," explained the sheriff. "Shucks, might not be until late tonight, then, now I calculate it."

Shifting his raincoat to the opposite arm, Early said, "If they took the ships, that means they were going some distance. Some place they could reach by air."

Sheriff Brown said, "I don't think they're going to get far."

"How come?"

"Reports I been getting in my car," said the sheriff, "there's a big sand storm blowing across a good part of this area. May even reach us here before long. Nobody's going to do much flying in weather like that, no matter what kind of fancy plane they got."

"Then maybe I still have a chance," said Early, brightening.

An agent in a dark suit and hat brought a coffee cup over to the poolside table where Early was sitting. "Try this, sir," he said, placing the cup in front of the young agent.

"Anybody should be able to make coffee, Collins," said Early.

"You haven't seen the machine they have here. It's for making five gallons at a time," said Collins. "On top of that, they don't use real coffee. This is a substitute made out of beans and dandelion greens."

Early's lips puckered as he took a sip. "Not bad."

"Taste, you know, is partly mental. If you pretend—"

"That's enough. Get back to work." Early leaned back in the sunchair. It was daylight now. The sand storm had never reached this far. The last reports indicated it had died over most of the desert a half-hour ago. "Awful," muttered Early, trying a little more of the coffee.

Another agent in a dark suit, this one taller

and leaner than the other one, came hurrying across to Early's table. "Something's come up, sir."

"What is it, Reisberson?"

"We just got a report relayed to our Manzana office by the Air Corps," said Reisberson. "They spotted a chariot."

Early got up. "Where?"

"It's down, that's the important part, down in the desert about thirty miles from here."

"Have they landed, taken a look at the thing?"

"Not yet. They wanted to hear what you want to do."

Early said, "Air Corps is mellowing, giving me first crack. Tell them I'm on my way. You have the exact location?"

"Yes, sir."

"I'm getting ahead of them," said Early. "It's possible I'll beat them."

"What, sir?"

Early didn't reply. He hurried off to arrange for transportation.

CHAPTER XXIII

Escapes

By the time Cole lifted the cockpit cover and scrambled out onto the pitted surface of the chariot, the low-flying Air Corps monoplane had ceased to circle. It was heading away from him.

He waved at its retreating tail. "Aren't you chaps going to pay a call?"

The plane continued to grow smaller in the now clear morning sky.

Cole sat down. "They've obviously reported us to somebody," he assumed. "So I can expect a rescue party of some description shortly."

The wind had piled sand up against the right side of the ship, half burying it. Cole stepped down to a fresh dune and scanned his surroundings.

To his left, about a mile off, were some lopsided joshua trees. All else was sand. "Make a splendid beach."

Cole judged, from the position of the already bright sun, that the time was about 9 A.M. He walked about a few yards from the downed craft.

"I wonder where everybody is? That storm must have prevented anyone from taking to the air. I doubt if even Richard—"

He heard another motor. An airplane was approaching.

"No shortage of rescuers, it seems. I'll wager that's Richard and Smitty now."

The plane was coming from the wrong direction for that, though. Perhaps they'd been circling. You couldn't be certain.

A biplane, a dark blue in color. They'd seen him, and the chariot, and were going to land.

Cole was about to wave, but something made him hesitate.

The plane landed about five hundred feet away, scattering streamers of sand.

A man with a machine gun dropped out of the passenger side of the plane before the propeller had ceased spinning. He started firing at Cole.

The door of their cell opened. A guard carrying a breakfast tray entered. There was a pot of coffee on the tray, two cups, two bowls of dry cereal, a pitcher of milk, silverware, one banana, and a .38 revolver. The revolver rested close to the guard's right hand. "I have brought you young ladies your morning meal," he announced.

"Stand by," Nellie said quietly out of the side of her mouth to Jennifer. She walked toward the tray-carrying guard.

"Please to stand back until I place—"

Nellie kicked. Her foot swung up incredibly high. The toe of her shoe hit the bottom of the tray dead center.

The hot coffee splashed back into the guard's face. The milk slurped up out of the pitcher and splotched the front of him. Cups and bowls clacked together, spun to the floor, and smashed.

Nellie ignored all that. Her eye was on the gun. And she got it before the man did.

"What have you done?" he yowled, both hands pressed over his burned face.

Cereal crackled under foot as Nellie reached out and caught the man's wrist with her left hand. "Over against the bunks, my friend."

"I'm injured, miss. I may be maimed for life, do you not—"

"On the bunk, sweetie, or your life won't last much beyond this morning."

"Nellie, maybe he is seriously hurt," said Jennifer, biting her thumb knuckle, watching the two of them.

"I doubt it."

"The young miss is right, I am mortally injured." The guard, hands still over his face, stumbled back against the bed. Unavoidably he sat down on it. "Just look."

Nellie hesitated a second, then crossed to him.

"See?" He dropped his hands and made a lunge for the gun.

Her foot snapped out again, not so high this time. "Malingerer," she said.

"Yow!" She'd caught him in the kneecap. He clutched at his knee with the hands he'd meant to use on her and the gun. He sat down again. "What a pity, what a pity. To hobble for the rest of my life."

"Over on your frontside," ordered Nellie.

"I'm too pained to move."

"Over." She caught his foot and half flipped him.

"Such unfeminine conduct," protested the guard, "for so small and sweet-seeming a young lady."

"Jenny," said Nellie, "take out his belt. Then tie his hands behind his back with it. Tight."

"Okay, Nellie. And then what?"

"Then we get out of here."

Cole spat out a mouthful of sand. He had managed to get on the other side of the chariot, with it standing between him and the man with the tommy gun.

Getting rid of the last of the sand he'd taken in while rolling and tumbling to this position of relative safety, Cole shouted to the man, "Let's negotiate, old fellow."

"We advise you to surrender." The pilot had joined the other man. "There is no possibility of escape."

"I have your good chum, Herr Dirks, here with me," lied Cole. "If you chaps don't give up, I'll be forced to blow his brains out."

There was silence, no more slugs, no further talk, for a full minute.

Then the pilot called out, "Go ahead, Mr. Wilson. We cannot be swayed by emotional blackmail."

"Cold-blooded rascals," said Cole to himself. He waited a few seconds before replying, in a fairly good imitation of Dirks's voice, "Hey, this guy ain't kidding. He's going to lay me out."

"We are sorry, Dirks."

"Aw, don't let him do it. Have a heart, you birds. Ain't we been pals and comrades in arms?"

"It is no use, we must take him in," shouted the pilot. "And we must quickly hide this fallen ship of yours."

"Oof," said Cole suddenly in his own voice. "Say old boy, you can't . . . oof."

"Take that, you wise-mouth jerk," he bellowed in the Dirks voice.

He thumped his fist against the side of the chariot and groaned.

Then he allowed a silence to ensue.

The machine-gunner took the bait. "Dirks, what's happened?"

Cole counted off ten seconds before answering. "I got the gun. He had the drop on me, but I decked him anyhow. Come on over and grab him."

They fell for it. Both of them came unsuspectingly around the chariot, the pilot with his revolver still in his belt holster, the machine-gunner with the weapon casually aimed at the sand.

"Never underestimate the power of illusion," said Cole, grinning, his borrowed automatic pointed at them.

CHAPTER XXIV

A Small Invasion

Early that morning, when the wind began to die and let the sand fall back to earth, the Avenger had opened the cockpit of the chariot he'd been piloting. A few yards away were the other two craft they'd borrowed from the Oasis's underground hangar.

Smitty popped up out of his craft next. "Are we ready to get back in the air, Dick?"

Turning away from the wind, the Avenger answered, "Yes, I think this is the last of the sand storm."

They had traveled about ten miles last night, with Benson's chariot in the lead, when the force of the wind and swirling sand had forced them to put down for the duration of the blow.

"We hae lost a good bit of precious time," observed Mac as he emerged into the morning.

"So has everyone else," reminded the Avenger.

Smitty came all the way out of his ship and slid down the top of the thing onto the sand. "Before we take off, Dick, I got to know what these guys have been up to. You asked most of the questions back there under the Oasis whilst me and Mac was mopping up."

"Out in the desert, some way beyond the place we're bound for," explained Benson, "is a large preserve of government land. No one is allowed near the area, not even the local law. No commercial or military flights are allowed to pass o er that ten-mile square."

"Some kind of government hush-hush government deal, huh?"

MacMurdie had joined Smitty next to Benson's ship. He scratched his chin, saying, "They must be testing something out of doors then, a new airplane, or maybe some kind of artillery piece."

"I think it's more important than that," said Benson. "None of the men I questioned with the truth gas knew the specifics. I suspect our government may be using this particular site to work on some kind of atomic weapon."

"Whoosh," exclaimed Mac, " 'tis the atomic bomb we've ourselves mixed up with?"

"You know an atom bomb is inevitable, Mac. And it will be either us or the Germans who get it first."

"Aye, though the English mot have a long-shot chance."

"Unlikely that either the British or the Russians are in a position to put forth the required effort now," said the Avenger.

Smitty said, "So that's what all this mumbo-jumbo is about, these flying chariots. To spy on this desert project."

"You'll notice each of these crafts is equipped to take aerial photos both day and night, Smitty."

The giant shook his head. "And Ralph must have run into one."

Benson nodded. "One of the men I questioned knew something about your friend's death, Smitty."

"You should have told me then, Dick. I'd like to have taken the—"

"The man himself wasn't responsible. It was apparently Danker himself, the head man, who was piloting the chariot in question," said the Avenger. "It had a temporary malfunction and was forced to land. Ralph Stevenson happened by at just that moment. He went to offer help. Danker didn't want help, he wanted anonymity. So he killed Ralph."

"How?"

"Some sort of poison gas was used," said Benson.

Smitty pressed his lips tight together and nearly closed his eyes. "Damn," he said at last. "Of all the stupid ways . . . it was just a coincidence that Ralph was there. He was trying to help and—"

"Take it easy, lad," said Mac, touching the big man's arm. "The world and its way kin be strange some times, lad."

Smitty took a deep breath. "Okay, let's get going." He pulled away from MacMurdie and stalked back to his ship.

"Smitty," called Benson.

128

"Yeah?" said the giant without turning around.

The Avenger watched Smitty's hunched back. "Nothing," he said.

"You were," said Jennifer in a whisper, "very effective with our guard, Nellie."

"Yep." The little blonde w s leading the way along a stone corridor. "That's the door to the place where they have the chariots stored."

"I've always thought of m self as being sort of stubborn and feisty," continued Jennifer, "but you—"

"I grew up a tomboy," said Nellie. "Now let's concentrate on getting out of this joint."

"Off we go into the wild bl e yonder," sang Cole as the commandeered airplane lifted off.

"I heard about you," said the pilot, who was tied up behind the seat. The machine-gunner, also tied, Cole had left behind, propped against the chariot.

"Yes, my notoriety seems to have spread from the rockbound coast of Maine to the sun-drenched shores of -"

"You're the guy with the big mouth."

"You didn't do so bad o n , old man, telling me all about how to get to your other secret hideaway."

"What choice did you give me? Either talk or get left to dry up in the desert. Or get eaten by wild animals."

"Let us fervently hope you told the truth. Otherwise . . . "

"I didn't lie."

Cole set the plane on the course the pilot had given him. "I notice you fellows don't go in for radios in your planes."

"We can't afford to get spotted that way. So there's absolutely no radio communication."

"How do you get landing instructions, then?"

"I don't. We got a lookout stationed up in a place in the rocks. He signals them to open up the underground hangar lid when he sees one of us."

"Ah, very efficient," said Cole, grinning. "In other words, my fallen Icarus, when this lookout sees our plane fast approaching he will signal them to open up and let us in?"

"Yeah, that's right."

"Very good," said Cole, patting the object on the seat next to him.

He'd left the machine-gunner behind, but brought the machine gun.

The cliffside opened. Three hovering chariots showed up in the bright midmorning.

Danker, a new pair of binoculars to his narrowed eyes, watched them. "What does this mean?"

"Trouble, Herr—sir," suggested Kurt.

"Those idiots should not be traveling in broad daylight."

"Perhaps there was some new trouble at the Oasis, which caused—"

"Shut up, you're another idiot." Danker lowered the glasses and slapped them against his leg.

One by one, the three disk-shaped craft dropped down through the opening. They landed side by side. Then sat there, no one emerging.

Danker had the binoculars up to his eyes again. "Who is that in the nearest ship? I can't quite make him out."

"It looks like Kraus, sir."

"No, it's not Kraus." Danker glanced around at the four armed men placed around the hangar. With his head turned sideways, he stroked his cheek for a moment. "I'll find out what these idiots are up to." He handed Kurt the glasses and went striding to the nearest newly landed chariot. "Have I not instructed you numerous times not to—"

All at once the Avenger was out of his cabin. He had his unique .22 pistol aimed at Danker. "Don't make a move," he said in his calm voice.

The thin, dark man's hand had been moving toward the gun at his side. He froze now. Not merely because of the gun the Avenger was holding on him, but because of the look in the other man's eyes. "You would be the Avenger, would you not?"

"Yes, I'm known as the Avenger."

Danker made a slight bow. "My name is Danker."

Smitty had his cockpit open. He heard the name and made an angry sound in his throat.

"You are audacious indeed," said Danker to Benson. "To brave the lion in his den, as it were."

"We can talk later, Danker," said Benson curtly. "Right now I want you to tell your men to drop their rifles and pistols."

Danker chuckled. "A ridiculous request," he said. "Especially since I hold your Miss Gra a

131

prisoner. She will be killed instantly unless you drop your own gun, Avenger."

"A bluff," said the Avenger. "One that isn't going to work."

"Oh, really? I have but to raise my hand and—"

"Don't let him kid you, Dick." Nellie, with Jennifer behind her, stood framed in the doorway which had just opened in the hangar wall.

Danker winced when he heard the voice behind him. "Idiots, a staff composed of nothing but idiots!"

But then Jennifer, watching what was going on between Danker and Benson, stumbled. She knocked Nellie down.

While the little blonde was still on her knees a guard with a pistol dived and pressed his gun to her side.

"Now, out of that ship, or I'll have her slaughtered before your eyes," said Danker.

Benson obliged, hopping to the hangar floor.

"Now I bid farewell to all you fools." Danker climbed into the chariot, closed the cockpit and less than a minute later the ship was rising up through the still open roof.

The man holding the gun on Nellie happened to let his eyes follow the ascent of Danker's getaway ship.

Nellie acted. She fell out flat, rolled sideways, and bowled the gunman over.

His gun went off, hitting no one. She kicked it from his hand before he could fire again.

"You okay, Nellie?" called out Smitty.

"Yes, you dope."

"Okay, I'll be seeing you soon." The giant slammed his own cockpit. He took off after Danker.

The Avenger raised his pistol. "The rest of you, your chief has run. It's time for you to quit."

They apparently agreed with him. Rifles and pistols clanged to the floor.

"I do not carry a gun, Herr Avenger," explained Kurt. "However, here is my knife." He threw it down.

Nellie got up and ran over to the Avenger. "Dick, where's Cole?" she asked. "Do you know?"

"Isn't he here?"

"No, the ship he was in never arrived," said the little blonde. "And because of a storm or something they didn't go looking for him and his pilot until this morning, I think."

Jennifer walked slowly over to them. "I'm sorry I almost messed things up for everybody," she apologized.

"This is Jennifer Hamblin," said Nellie. "Do you have any word about her uncle?"

"Yes, do you?"

Benson said "He's fine, Miss Hamblin. He's on his way to recovering from the drugs Danker used on him. I'd guess that by now he's safely back in Manzana. Don Early's no doubt seen to that."

"Will he . . . I mean, they don't think he's a traitor?"

"We explained some of it to the sheriff by phone last night, lass," said Mac, who had dis-

133

embarked from his flying machine. "I dinna think there'll be any trouble. Though he mot have to answer a good lot of questions."

"I knew . . . I was certain he wouldn't have joined them on his own."

Nellie was looking glum. "Seems like everybody's okay except Cole."

"Yer not supposed to be any great fan of his, Nell," reminded MacMurdie.

"I don't have to be enamored of somebody to worry about them," said Nellie. "I'm worried about Smitty, too. What's he going to try to do?"

"Bring back Danker," said the Avenger.

"It appears Danker is the one who killed Smitty's friend," explained Mac.

"This has all been—" began Nellie.

An airplane engine sounded overhead.

"Not an Air Corps ship," said Benson.

"Excuse me," volunteered Kurt. "It is one of our planes, Herr—sir. The one which went to hunt for Dirks and the young man this lady is interested in so much."

"I hope they found him," said Jennifer.

Instead of coming down for a landing, the plane suddenly climbed. It went roaring perpendicularly up until it had gained considerable altitude. Then it executed a loop-the-loop, came diving down for the opening, pulled up short of it, and looped away again.

"Do ye know," said Mac, watching the stunting plane, "I would nae be surprised if Cole himself were at the controls of that thing."

"Why doesn't he just land, then?" said Nellie impatiently. "This is no time for showing off."

The plane came back, killed its engine, and glided down through the opening. It touched

134

down on the hangar floor, bounced once, rolled almost to the far stone wall, and then stopped.

Half a minute later Cole got out of the ship, grinning at them all. "Hello," he said, "my name is Corrigan. Is this Los Angeles?"

"Must you always be such a . . . such an idiot?" said Nellie. Despite her anger, she ran up to him and gave him a hug.

"Ah, pixie," he said, "I suspect you've had too much desert sun, to be acting in such a sentimental—"

"Nerts," said Nellie, letting go. "You're impossible." She turned away, walked a few steps, then turned back to face him. "But I was worried about you, Cole, and I'm happy you're alive."

"I share your sentiments." He looked around the hangar. "Where's Smitty?"

"The lad took off after Danker," said Mac, "the both of them a-flying in chariots, no less."

"So that's who I saw," said Cole. He held out his hand to Benson. "I take it we're coming to the conclusion of this case, Richard."

"Very shortly," answered Benson.

"I hope so, since I'm considerably anxious to find out what it's all about," said Cole.

"Some answers,". said the Avenger, "we may never get."

CHAPTER XXV

Dogfight

Smitty shortened the distance between himself and the escaping Danker as they droned along a few hundred feet above the desert.

He knew the disk-ship he was flying would travel faster than the one he was chasing. During the long wait for the storm to subside, the giant had gotten to tinkering with the craft. He'd made—just for the fun of it then—a few changes. One such resulted in the increased speed he was getting now.

Danker was heading farther out over the desert, away from Manzana.

"He's only got enough fuel for a short haul," reflected Smitty. "These babies only carry enough for a few hours' flying time, and Dick's already used some of that one's."

Up ahead of him, about a quarter-mile now,

Danker's ship made a sudden sideways move, gaining altitude.

"Doggone, I think this guy's looking for a fight."

Danker's chariot was coming back, high to Smitty's left.

The small observation planes were not fixed up with any kind of weapons, Smitty knew that.

But at such a low altitude Danker could open his cockpit. He did now, when he was above the giant's disk.

A slug whammed against the upper surface of the chariot.

"Hot dog, this is just like the Lafayette Escadrille dogfights I been reading about in the pulp mags," said Smitty.

He caused his ship to make a snapping half loop. This brought him up over Danker. Then Smitty dropped the craft. His ship bumped Danker's. Bumped it again.

There was a crackling sound from down under. "Hope that's part of him and not part of me."

Smitty climbed away.

Circling back, he saw that Danker's cockpit cover had burst in half.

The thin, dark man sent another pistol shot at him.

Smitty headed right down for him. "Show you something about tiddlywinks," he said.

The lip of his chariot came down on the rim of the other man's disk.

Danker's ship flipped over in the air, began spinning.

Before Danker could get control of it, the ship smashed downside-first into the sand.

Going down lower, Smitty circled the wreck.

He saw Danker come struggling out of the ruin of the chariot on all fours. The man tottered to his feet and shook a fist a Smitty. Then he raised the pistol, but before he could fire any more, he passed out and collapsed on the sand.

"I kept my word, Ralph," said Smitty aloud. "I got the guy who did it." He landed his chariot. "Now I'll turn him over to the law.

Don Early was wearing his raincoat, although it wasn't raining. "I think I'm getting a cold," he said to Richard Benson. "I keep feeling very chilly."

The two men met in front of the sheriff's office in Manzana. "These desert nights can do that," said Benson.

"Wanted to thank you," said the government agent, "for lending a hand."

"It was Smitty's idea, really," said the Avenger, "our getting into this business."

"It helped us out. Those damn chariots had been eluding me for weeks."

"I suppose," said Benson, glancing up at the hot afternoon sky, "you can't tell me what it is those foreign agents were trying to photograph."

"Right, I can't," said Early. "Pretty important, though."

"Very well, no further questions about that," said Benson. "Although I would like to know what's going to happen to Dr. Hamblin."

"Was just talking to his niece about him over at the hospital," said the young agent. "Hamblin will be released in a few days. Doesn't look like there'll be any long-range damage to his mind, though he may be a little fuzzy for a bit. Got a specialist in from Los Angeles."

"Will he be allowed to return home with Jennifer?"

Early buttoned the top button of his raincoat. "People in Washington are going to want to talk to him, but he's not going to be locked up or anything," he said. "By the end of the month he should be back in Boston. With a few extra people keeping an eye on him. We don't want anyone else going into the chariot business."

Benson nodded. "And Danker?"

"He's a big one. I have to admit I had no idea he was even in this country, let alone right underfoot," said Agent Early. "He'll be tried for espionage, the works."

"Good," said the Avenger. "We'll be leaving tomorrow."

Early watched him for a few seconds. "Going back to Manhattan, are you?"

"Yes, to our New York City offices."

Early ran a palm over his closecut hair. "Not going any place else? Mean, you wouldn't be making a side trip to, say, Arizona or New Mexico?"

"Not at all," answered Benson. "Is that where you're heading next?"

"Can't tell you that," said Early. "But I'm happy to hear you're all going to be in New York for a while."

"Yes, our paths aren't likely to cross for some time."

Early smiled a relieved smile.

CHAPTER XXVI

Blessed Event

It started raining when they were a block from the Manhattan hospital. Cole unfurled the umbrella he'd been swinging like a cane. "Rain. You remember rain, don't you, princess?"

Nellie said, "Vaguely. Although a few days in that desert out there can make you forget."

"Which reminds me," said Cole, grinning, "now that we're back in the concrete canyons of Gotham, you can start being your old unsentimental self again. I know that in California you showed a surprising concern for my fate, but it was—"

"Stop," she said. "Let's forget about that and concentrate on our visit with Josh and Rosabel."

They climbed up the steps of the glass-and-red-brick hospital. Cole shut the umbrella, shook it off, and opened a door for the little blonde.

140

Before they could inquire of the nurse at the reception desk, Josh came hurrying down a side hallway toward them.

"Hey, good to see you," the black man said.

Nellie surveyed him. "Yes, you look very fatherly, Josh."

"Figure I would, I feel very paternal." He took each of them by the arm. "They're doing something or other with the babies. So you can't see Rosabel or them for a few minutes. We can wait in this waiting room down here."

When there were in the dim-lit room, sharing it with a nervous man with an unlit cigar in his mouth, Cole said, "Nellie and I had to call off our bet."

"About what?" asked Josh. He picked up copies of the *Herald Tribune*, the *Journal-American*, and the *Post*. "Want to read something while we wait? No? Just as well, they're a couple days old anyhow. What bet?"

"Pay him no mind," said Nellie. "It's only another of his inappropriate jests."

"She's trying to maintain it was a joke, but we were both serious," said Cole. "We had a small bet as to whether you would become the parent of a boy or a girl."

Josh laughed. "Well, see . . . you both won."

The man with the cigar put down the six-week-old copy of *Collier's* he'd been staring at. "Did you say you got a way to tell in advance whether it'll be a boy or a girl?"

Cole glanced at him. "Still waiting for yours to arrive?"

"Yeah, and it would be nice if it was a girl. Otherwise, we got to name him Junius."

"I'm sorry to inform you that we don't have

141

any system," said Cole. "I had a maiden aunt who claimed eighty percent infallibility in that area of prognostication with the use of tea leaves, but she neglected to pass the method on to me."

"Oh, we already tried tea leaves," said the man with the cigar. He returned to his magazine.

"Have you and Rosabel decided on names yet?" asked Nellie.

Josh shook his head. "Nope, though I think we're maybe getting close on the girl. It's funny, now I see the pair of them . . . none of the names we had picked out in advance seem to fit, quite."

"Be thankful you don't have to name one Junius," said Cole.

"You'll like them," said Josh, smiling. "I know everybody says this, but those two kids are really something. The boy recognizes me already. Yeah, when the nurse holds him up behind the glass, you can see he knows me." He rubbed his hands together and smiled again at Nellie and Cole. "I hear you had quite a time out there, huh? Smitty and Mac were telling me when they dropped by last night."

Nellie frowned. "Hasn't Richard been here yet?"

"Well, no," said Josh. "I figure, you know, he's got too much on his mind. I don't expect him to—"

Tiny bells jingled out in the corridor. Then the Avenger entered, carrying a teddy bear, two rattles, a rubber ball, and a green-paper-wrapped bouquet of yellow roses. "Congratulations, Josh," he said. "I brought over a few things."

"Well," said Josh, "that's very nice."

142

KENNETH ROBESON'S

DON'T MISS A BOOK IN THIS THRILLING SERIES!
NOW AT YOUR BOOKSTORE.

 A Warner Communications Company

KENNETH ROBESON'S

the Avenger

DON'T MISS A BOOK IN THIS THRILLING SERIES!
NOW AT YOUR BOOKSTORE.